Her heart ⎯⎯⎯⎯⎯⎯ nst the wall of her
chest as she rac⎯⎯⎯⎯⎯⎯⎯ ay. Stumbling, she
reached out for ⎯⎯⎯⎯⎯⎯⎯ lf. She paused for a
second, her ears pricked to any sounds.

Nothing.

For a moment she leaned heavily against the wall,
feeling its c⎯⎯⎯⎯
nearly chok⎯⎯⎯
freely down⎯⎯⎯
the wetness ⎯⎯

This ca⎯⎯

She sw⎯⎯
job. I shou⎯⎯
her, making⎯⎯

The flo⎯⎯
wall, she lu⎯⎯

I have ⎯⎯

She rea⎯⎯
first two ste⎯⎯
She squeeze⎯⎯
her.

That ⎯⎯

Expe⎯⎯
banister a⎯⎯
quick, yet⎯⎯
the moor⎯⎯
threatenec⎯⎯

Some⎯⎯
losing he⎯⎯
teetered, ⎯⎯

Then⎯⎯

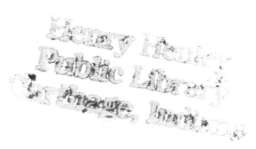

K.C. Oliver

Pretty Pretty

Echelon Press

Echelon Press
56 Sawyer Circle #354
Memphis, TN 38103

Copyright © 2005 by K. Sawchuk
ISBN: 1-59080-253-5
Library of Congress Control Number: 2005927343
www.echelonpress.com

First Echelon Press paperback printing: August 2005

Cover Art © Nathalie Moore
2005 Arianna Best In category Award winner

Printed in USA

Dedication

This book is dedicated to my late father "Oli".

This one's for you, daddy.

Acknowledgment

To my family and close friends for all the love and support they have given me right from the start: Mick, Joshua, Kara, RuthAnn, Carrie, Richard, Noreen, Cassie, Jenni, Louise, Dyanne, Valerie, and all the rest of my family and friends. I love you guys!

To my fantastic and supportive publisher Karen Syed, and my excellent editors Emily Carmain and Kat Thompson. Together we made this book come alive!

Finally, to the many sources (there are too many to mention!) who were extremely helpful in my research. If there are any discrepancies or errors within this story, they are my own and done to further the fictional story. Thank you all!

Prologue

Her heart pounded furiously against the wall of her chest as she raced down the long hallway. Stumbling, she reached out for the wall, steadying herself. She paused for a second, her ears pricked to any sounds.

Nothing.

For a moment she leaned heavily against the wall, feeling its coolness against her hot face. Fear clung to her, nearly choking her with its cloying scent. Sweat trickled freely down her forehead, burning her eyes. She swiped at the wetness with the back of her hand.

This can't be happening. Monsters do not *exist!*

She swallowed hard. *I never should have taken this job. I should have listened to everyone.* A sob tore through her, making her throat ache and burn.

The floor creaked, startling her. Pushing away from the wall, she lurched forward, her feet feeling like lead weights.

I have to keep moving. Don't look back.

She reached the stairs, sliding and tripping down the first two steps before grabbing the banister to right herself. She squeezed her eyes shut as dizzying relief washed over her.

That was close. Too close!

Pretty, Pretty

Expelling a ragged breath, she clung tightly to the banister as she began down the marble staircase, her steps quick, yet careful. The white of the marble glowed eerily in the moonlight, and she swallowed back the fear that threatened to overtake her again.

Something touched her shoulder. She spun around, losing her balance. For what seemed like an eternity, she teetered, her arms flailing in the air for any handhold.

Then she began to fall.

In a blur, she tumbled and rolled down the staircase. A sickening crack filled the air, followed by a sharp cry. A splash of red tainted the glaring whiteness of the marble.

Then silence.

She whimpered and tried to move, but pain knifed through her, holding her in place. Trembling with terror, she watched as a shadowy figure drew closer. She tried to move again, dragging herself slowly, painfully. The figure stepped in front of her, blocking any further escape.

With great effort, the girl's gaze traveled up the darkly covered torso to a hooded face. The head lifted; the hood slipped back. An odd musty smell filled the air, making her gag. She began to cry softly as the cloaked form moved closer.

"So pretty," the figure rasped. "So pretty." It reached out to touch her face. "So pretty."

The girl on the floor shuddered as something cold and clammy touched her cheek. She tried to pull away, but a wave of dizziness washed over her, and a strange rushing noise filled her ears, shutting out all other sounds. Her body began to twitch in a fit of convulsions. Blood trickled from her lips, pooling on the floor.

The shadowy figure watched silently.

Then the darkness came, both comforting and frightening. For a few seconds, the girl on the floor fought against it, using the last of her strength to fight for survival. Then, too tired, she let herself be drawn into the darkness. Suddenly a blinding light exploded in the centre of all the black. It felt warm. It felt good. A small smile touched her lips, and with a final shuddering breath, she lay still.

The figure cocked its head and stared at the unmoving girl on the floor. Then it reached out to touch her again, stroking the girl's dark hair. "So pretty...so pretty...so pretty..."

One

A hard jolt, followed by a screech, jarred eighteen-year-old Quinn Hunter awake. "Are we there already?" Quinn asked sleepily, rubbing her unusual, violet colored eyes with her fists.

Her best friend, Holly Gates, also eighteen, glanced at Quinn and cocked a blonde eyebrow. "Already? We left Los Angeles five and a half hours ago." Holly pasted an annoyed look on her pretty face. "Not that you would have noticed. Your snoring kept the entire plane awake."

"I don't snore," Quinn whispered harshly, all the while gingerly peeking around.

"Why don't you just ask that cute guy over there with the dark circles under his eyes?" Holly flipped her long blonde hair over her shoulder, her deep blue eyes dancing with mischief.

Quinn dared a glance at the guy in question, but wasn't about to ask him if she'd been snoring.

Holly unclipped her belt as the jet came to a complete stop. "You coming?" she asked, as she reached overhead to get her carry-on bag.

Quinn sent her friend a droll look. "Nah, figured I'd just hang around here. I've got a comfy chair and all the pretzels I can eat. It's heaven, I tell ya."

Holly pulled down a black bag and a hot pink one, and put them both at her feet. "Aren't you *ever* serious?"

Quinn shrugged. "And confuse you?"

Holly considered this. "You're right. I would think aliens stole my best friend and left me with you."

"There ya go."

The girls followed the other passengers to the jetway, and slowly filed out. Inside the airport terminal, a woman with garlands of flowers draped over her arm walked up to them.

"Miss Gates and Miss Hunter?"

Holly smiled and nodded. "Yes."

"Aloha," she greeted in a voice as smooth as honey. She placed a garland around Holly's neck, then Quinn's, giving them each a peck on the cheek.

Quinn picked up the pretty pink-flowered garland between her fingers, brought it to her nose, and sniffed.

Holly gave her an odd look. "You are truly strange, Hunter."

"These garlands are so beautiful, and smell even better."

Holly chuckled. "They're called *leis*, Quinn. We get them as part of our flight package. Didn't you read any of the books I gave you?"

Quinn shook her head, making her dark curls bob. "Didn't have time."

"Well, anyway, when you get home you can tell everyone you got *leied* in Hawaii."

Quinn laughed. "I like that. Do you think I can get that on a T-shirt?"

Holly rolled her eyes. "Probably in every store on

Maui." She glanced around and then added, "Come on, let's get going. Mr. Barrington said he wouldn't be able to pick us up, so we have to catch a taxi."

They waited by the luggage carousel for their bags. For some reason, Quinn missed her bag and they had to wait for it to make another revolution. Holly grumbled, not able to figure out how someone could miss a bright pink suitcase, but Quinn only smiled and shrugged.

Outside, three taxis were parked by the curb. Holly and Quinn walked toward one, and the driver got out of his cab.

"Aloha, ladies," he called. He took their bags and placed them in the trunk, then hurried to open the back door for them. They climbed in.

He slid in behind the wheel, then turned around to face them. "Where can I take you, ladies?" His teeth flashed white against his darkly tanned face.

"Barrington House, please," Holly said.

The man's smile faltered then died. "Barrington House?"

Holly and Quinn glanced at each other. Then Holly pulled out a map and placed her finger on a point between Lahaina and Kaanapali. "It's located ri–"

"I know where it is," he interrupted, frowning. "Are you sure that's were you want to go? I mean, there are a lot of great hotels in the area that are much nicer. Even cheaper–"

"That's quite all right," Quinn cut in. "We're not here for a vacation. We're here to work. We have jobs waiting for us at Barrington House."

A strange look came over the man's face before he

finally faced forward and started up the cab. He didn't speak to them again during the ride to Barrington House. He didn't even drive up to the hotel, stopping instead on the edge of the highway.

As he began to unload their luggage onto the side of the road, Holly jumped out of the cab and hurried over to him. "You need to take us all the way to the hotel. Mr. Barrington is going to take care of the fare."

Quinn got out of the vehicle to see what the problem was, just as the driver got back in. Without a backward glance, he sped off.

"Strange," Quinn commented, watching the cab until it disappeared from sight. "Didn't he want his fare?"

"Guess not." Holly shrugged. "Who cares? It's his loss. We're in Hawaii. What more could a couple of girls want?"

"How about a valet to carry our bags?" Quinn commented dryly.

Holly rolled her blue eyes as she picked up her suitcases and started up the long driveway. Quinn gathered her luggage and followed.

"Have you read the Lynne Arthur book, *Eyes of a Killer*, yet?" Holly called over her shoulder to Quinn. "I really enjoyed it."

Quinn caught up to her as Holly began to tell her what she thought about the Arthur book. Quinn listened quietly, marveling at her friend's ability to analyze the books she read. Someday Holly wanted to write books of her own, and she would probably be great at it.

As they rounded a bend, the hotel loomed in front of them. "It's beautiful," Holly commented breathlessly, stopping to look at the huge, light-gray, three-story building. It resembled an old plantation house. A sturdy wooden balcony with fancy black wrought iron railing spanned the entire length of the front of the building. Each suite had a pair of French doors with beautiful beveled glass; and for privacy, the balcony was partitioned along its length with gracefully carved, thick wooden slabs.

Quinn cocked her head to the side thoughtfully. "It reminds me of the kind of house you'd read about in one of your mystery novels. All we need is for it to be dark and stormy."

Holly seemed mesmerized by the house. "Yeah, I know. Isn't it great?"

Quinn shook her head. "Hol, you need to get a life."

"A life? I don't want just one. As a writer, I can create as many different lives as I want. And I plan to have plenty." With those words, Holly skipped up the gray stone steps.

Quinn held back a second and looked up at the house again. She shuddered. The house gave her the creeps. Then high up on the third floor; something moved.

A curtain?

Quinn stared hard at the window where she thought she'd seen movement.

Was someone watching them?

"Are you coming?" Holly called, startling her.

Quinn shook off the strange sensation. Someone had probably heard voices and was just checking it out.

"Yeah, I'm coming," she returned, and headed up the steps as Holly opened the door.

The air conditioning felt cool against her skin as they walked up to the reception desk. No one was there.

"May I help you?" a deep voice said from behind them.

They spun around. Both girls blinked as they took in the appearance of the older man. He had a shock of white hair, and his skin seemed almost transparent. His eyes were faded blue, but they were sharp. Now *he* looked like something out of a mystery novel.

Quinn snapped her mouth shut, and cleared her throat. "Ah...I'm Quinn Hunter, and this is Holly Gates," Quinn said. She gestured awkwardly toward Holly. "We were hired to work here."

The man's bushy white eyebrows rose, and he smiled. "Of course, of course, the girls from Los Angeles."

Quinn swallowed hard. This place was definitely giving her the creeps. Quinn glanced at Holly, she was smiling. How could she be taking this all so casually?

"Allow me to introduce myself," he said, interrupting Quinn's thoughts. "I'm Edward Barrington, and this–" he began, looking past their shoulders, "is my sister, Edith Barrington."

Quinn turned and stared at the white-haired lady who had crept up. She was the spitting image of Mr. Barrington, except she wore her hair in a bun. And she moved as silently as a cat.

Holly stepped forward to shake their hands and express her pleasure to be here, while Quinn suppressed an urge to shudder again.

What was wrong with her?

Forcing her feet to move, she wiped her sweaty hand

on her beige shorts and shook her employers' hands, too. "Thank you for inviting us to work here," she said, making herself smile.

"And we're happy to have you," Edith said in a soft voice.

"Now," Edward put in, "why don't you show the girls to their room, Edith?"

She smiled at her brother. "Yes, yes, of course." She headed for a huge marble staircase. "This way, girls."

Picking up their bags, they followed the older woman up the stairs. Quinn glanced back at Mr. Barrington and inhaled sharply. He was studying them intensely, but the moment their eyes made contact, his face softened and he smiled at her. She returned his smile with a faltering one, then willed her feet to continue up the stairs, her shoes feeling like they were filled with lead weights. All the way up the stairs, she could feel his gaze boring into her back.

Edith took them to the second floor and turned right, leading them almost to the end of the hall before she stopped in front of a closed door. "This will be your room," she said as she opened the door. Inside, they could see that the room faced the back of the inn. "I hope you girls don't mind sharing."

"Not at all," Quinn spoke up, exceedingly glad that she wouldn't be alone in this creepy place. She just couldn't shake the queer feeling fluttering in her stomach.

"Good," Edith returned. "Why don't you both get settled, then come down for lunch? The kitchen is on the main floor, just to the right of the staircase. With all the noise, you can't miss it. I'll explain your duties then, all right?"

The girls nodded.

As soon as the door was shut, Holly burst out, "This place is awesome!"

Quinn tossed her suitcases onto the bed that was closest to the balcony, and sat down beside them. "Yeah, great," she replied dryly.

Holly glanced at Quinn. "What's wrong?"

"I don't know," Quinn admitted. "It's just a feeling."

"A bad one?"

Quinn nodded. "Real bad."

Holly shook her head as she tossed her luggage on the bed near the door. "You know, if you'd get your nose out of those psych books and just read something ordinary, maybe you wouldn't be so paranoid."

"I'm studying to be a psychiatrist, Hol. At any rate, what kind of books would you rather I read? Mystery? Then for sure I'd be paranoid." Quinn smiled as Holly harrumphed.

"At least you'd have reason to be paranoid. Instead, all you do is pick apart everything and everyone. You're always looking for..." Holly floundered for the right word, then just said, "something."

Quinn shrugged. "I'm observant."

Holly frowned at her friend. "Yeah, and that's great, but do you have to always analyze everything?"

"You analyze others' writing," Quinn pointed out.

"That's different, and I don't always look for the bad."

Quinn couldn't respond to that. She didn't always look for the bad in everything, did she? Quinn watched silently as Holly unpacked. Holly opened the top two drawers of the dresser and laid her clothes neatly inside. She pulled out a few plastic hangers from a pouch just inside the top of her suitcase, draped the dressier things she'd brought over the hangers, then went to the closet.

Quinn turned her attention toward the glass doors and gazed at the ocean in the distance. Maybe she'd jumped the gun a little with the bad feeling. So what if the house was monstrous, old, and creepy. And, so what, if the owners could be the relatives of the Addams family. She would give this place a chance.

Suddenly, a loud screech rent the air. Quinn jumped up from the bed just in time to see Holly fall.

Two

Holly hit the floor with a bone-jarring thud, then shielded her face as a screeching cat flew out at her and landed hard on her chest before disappearing under the bed in a flurry of black and white fur.

Quinn bit back a laugh as she went to her friend's side. "Are you all right?" she asked as she gave Holly a hand up.

Holly glanced balefully in the cat's direction; the animal peeked at them from under Holly's bed. "That crazy cat just scared ten years off my life!"

Quinn giggled.

"It's not funny, Quinn. I was totally freaked." She rubbed her hand over a sore spot on her chest. "And that cat weighs a ton, too!"

Quinn burst out laughing.

"*Quinn*," Holly cried.

"You–you–should have seen...your face," Quinn managed between gasps, before she dissolved into giggles again.

Holly grudgingly began to smile, too. "I guess I must have looked pretty funny."

Quinn nodded, still laughing.

"But it's not *that* funny."

Pretty, Pretty

Quinn forced herself to maintain control as she wiped the tears from her eyes. "I didn't think anything scared you, Hol."

Holly cast a disgusted glance at her friend. "I'd like to see how you would respond to a shrieking ball of fur attacking you."

Quinn bit her lip, trying to keep a straight face. "I don't think the cat was attacking you, Holly. I think you scared away one of its nine lives."

Holly laughed in spite of herself as she picked up the clothes she'd dropped during the attack of the fur ball. She hung them up in the closet, but not before taking a quick peek to see if there were any other surprises inside.

Returning to her bed, Holly shut her large suitcase and opened the smaller one next to it. She rummaged through it and pulled out her makeup, hair care items, and other accessories, and laid them out on a vanity table with a beveled mirror and matching chair. She left half the vanity clear for Quinn's things.

Quinn, in the meantime, had finally begun to unpack her own suitcases. She was nearly finished when there was a knock at the door. Quinn glanced at Holly, frowning.

Holly went to open the door. "Miss Barrington," Holly remarked in surprise. "We were just about to come down to the kitchen."

The woman smiled at her. "There's no hurry, girls."

At that moment, the cat tore out from under the bed and through Holly's legs in its attempt to gain freedom. Holly grasped the doorframe to steady herself and scowled after the feline. "Crazy cat," she muttered.

"Yes, Buttons has always been a bit of a flake."

Holly glanced at the older woman, biting her lip with guilt. "I didn't mean to insult your animal."

"Oh, pooh," she said with a wave of her wrinkled hand. "Buttons is Edward's cat, but even he thinks the animal is only good for violin strings."

Holly laughed, and Quinn politely followed suit.

"Was there something you wanted, Miss Barrington?" Quinn asked as she came up behind Holly.

"Want? Oh, heavens, no." The older woman chortled. "I just came up to see how you were doing, and if you liked the room."

"Everything is wonderful, Miss Barrington," Holly interjected. "But I'm curious, our taxi driver acted strangely when we asked him to drive us here. Why is that?"

Quinn winced at Holly's bluntness. Couldn't the girl ever keep her mouth shut? Holly could blurt out whatever was on her mind, whenever. If the Queen of England was in a parade and had toilet paper stuck to her shoe, Holly would stop the woman and tell her right then and there. But as unorthodox as Holly was, she did have a point, and Quinn wanted to know the answer to the question, too.

"People around here are superstitious. An ugly rumor gets started and everyone gets crazy." The older woman paused a moment, looking at them with piercing blue eyes, then said, "There is no truth to the rumor, and as long as you believe that, everything will be all right."

Quinn blinked. Did she just threaten them?

"Ready, Quinn? Quinn?"

Holly's voice cut into Quinn's thoughts. It took her a

moment to realize that she and Holly were alone again. Miss Barrington had left, and Quinn hadn't even acknowledged it.

"I'm sorry, Hol. What did you say?"

"I asked if you were ready to go down for lunch."

Quinn glanced at Holly, curious. Had Holly heard the threat, too, or had Quinn imagined it?

"Quinn?" Holly called, giving her an *Is-there-anybody-home?* look.

Quinn pushed the thoughts away. "Right. Let's go."

When they got downstairs, they quickly found the kitchen by following Miss Barrington's instructions. Standing in the center of an immaculate kitchen, they were startled when Edith bustled through a swinging door that separated the dining room from the kitchen.

"Ah, here you are." She went to check on something in a huge black pot and then came over to them. "Would you girls like some chicken stew?"

"That would be great," Holly spoke up.

"Just have a seat over there and I'll bring it over," Edith said, and pointed to a small table in the corner. "We prefer the staff to eat in the kitchen. I hope you don't mind."

"Not at all," Holly said as she sat down.

"Would you like some fresh bread, too?" Edith asked.

"That sounds wonderful, Miss Barrington," Quinn answered, finally speaking up.

Within moments, three bowls of steaming chicken stew were set on the table, with a plate of sliced, fresh bread and a server of butter. Edith set a glass of milk in front of each girl, and a cup of black coffee for herself.

Miss Barrington sat down, and took a quick sip of her coffee. "I hope you don't mind my joining you, but I thought it would be a good time to chat about your duties. Kind of like killing two birds with one stone, eh?" She chuckled as she picked up her spoon and dug into the stew.

They ate in silence for a few moments before Edith spoke up again. "Edward and I will expect one of you to handle the front desk and switchboard, while the other will handle the housekeeping, kitchen, and laundry duties. You will alternate weekly. I hope this won't be a problem."

"Not at all. We have performed similar duties at another hotel in the past."

"Very good," Edith said with a huge smile. "Our last girl–" Her smile was cut short just as quickly as her words, and she immediately changed the subject. "I'm sure our guests will love you."

Quinn spoke up. "How many guests are here now, Miss Barrington?"

Her blue eyes darted nervously around for a moment before her gaze settled on her cup. She took a sip, and then answered, "We had one last night, but he left this morning. But don't you worry," she went on brightly, "it's the low season." She got up suddenly, picking up her half-empty bowl and cup. "Finish up, girls. Then to get the feel of things, I'd like you to tidy the rooms on the second floor. Idle hands make idle minds." Her voice was singsong.

Quinn watched Miss Barrington as she bustled about, then the older woman left the kitchen. Quinn glanced at

Holly.

"Don't even start, Quinn," Holly cut in, just as Quinn opened her mouth. "There is nothing going on. There is nothing strange. There is nothing to worry about. Got me?"

Quinn blinked, shocked by Holly's outburst. "Okay." But she was anything but okay. She just couldn't help it, she had a bad feeling. And even though she said she'd give this place a chance, she was also going to be cautious. Even if she had to keep her thoughts to herself.

As soon as the girls finished their meal, Edith supplied them with a cart full of cleaning supplies and linens. Standing alone on the second floor, the girls glanced at each other.

"Well, are you ready to earn your keep?" Holly asked, grabbing a duster and a broom. "You take the room behind you, Quinn. And I'll take the one across the hall." Holly knocked on the closed door. "Maid service," Holly called out. She smiled devilishly at Quinn, and then disappeared into the room.

Quinn took a deep breath, grabbed another feather duster and broom, and then did the same as Holly, calling out, "Maid service" before going inside. It wasn't necessary, as there weren't any guests, but it was good practice.

Quinn stopped the moment she stepped into the room, surprised at the sight that greeted her. The room looked as if it hadn't been used in years. A layer of dust covered everything. Even cobwebs hung in the corners.

"This can't be right," she murmured, walking slowly around the room. Quinn thought about getting Holly, but quickly dismissed it. She'd think that Quinn was being paranoid again.

So the room hadn't been cleaned in a while. Big deal. Right? The bad feeling reared its ugly head again.

"Stop it. Just stop it," she ordered herself. She returned to the cart to grab a bucket and a sponge. The dust in that room required more than a feather duster.

A few hours later, Quinn and Holly returned to their own room, exhausted.

"I can't believe how dirty those rooms were," Holly exclaimed. She rubbed the back of her hand across her forehead, and left behind a dark smudge. "Out of twelve rooms, only five were actually clean. And that count includes ours."

"Well, Miss Barrington did say it was the low season," Quinn put in tiredly.

"Low season? You've got to be kidding. I'd say *no* season." Holly stomped over to the vanity and grabbed her shampoo, conditioner, and soap. "I'm going to take a shower." She disappeared through a small door that held an even smaller bathroom. Holly slammed the door behind her.

Quinn sighed, and then sneezed. She groaned; she felt filthy. She hoped Holly didn't decide to have a long shower. Quinn wandered over to the French doors that led to the balcony, and gazed out at the ocean.

A scraping sound startled her.

"Holly?" she called out. Quinn went over to the bathroom door. She could hear the water running, and Holly singing something about raindrops falling on her head.

The noise grated again. Quinn's eyes slowly moved toward the ceiling. It was above her; on the third floor. The noise was louder this time, and it was followed by a whimpering sound.

Heading into the hallway, Quinn was drawn to a narrow door that was ajar. It was the last door on the opposite side of the hallway. Quinn and Holly had assumed it was a closet. And it hadn't been open earlier. Had it?

She glanced inside. What should have been a back wall to the closet was actually another door, and she could see a small set of stairs through the opening. Quinn hesitated for a moment before cautiously going up.

The stairs were old, but in relatively good repair, as though someone had maintained them. The area was dimly lit, the only light source being the soft glow given off by a bulb just beyond the top landing.

As she reached the top, a hallway, smaller than the one below, opened up in front of her. She counted six rooms with closed doors. Three faced the front of the inn, and three faced the back.

"Hello?" she called warily. "Is someone up here?" She moved slowly down the hall, her footsteps echoed sharply in the silence. Quinn glanced down. The floor was spotlessly clean. "Strange," she muttered, her eyes missing nothing.

She reached the door of the room just above hers. Cautiously, she turned the knob and the door opened without a sound. As she pushed it wider, a sudden, sharp wail filled the air.

Something whipped past her, brushing against her

leg. Quinn screamed and jumped backward.

Buttons stopped at the head of the small stairway, crouched down, and hissed at her.

Quinn glared at the cat. "Stupid cat." Buttons made a strange growl-meow deep in his throat as she stepped up to him. "You know, I could drop-kick you right now," she warned the animal. The cat just stared up at her with startling green eyes.

An unseen, shrouded figure silently crept up behind Quinn. A darkly covered hand extended outward; the fingers twitched in anticipation. A mouth moved silently, repeating something over and over.

Buttons suddenly reared up again, hissing.

Quinn made a disgusted face. "Hiss to you, too, you demented fur-ball," she muttered, and then with an exasperated sigh, scooped Buttons up into her arms and went back downstairs.

The figure's hand remained in the air where Quinn's head had been only seconds before. The figure cocked its head; a strange whimpering filled its throat. Then the words, "Pretty...so pretty," were whispered into the silence.

As soon as Quinn and the cat were back on the second floor, Buttons squirmed out of her arms and tore off down the hall, disappearing down the stairs to the main floor.

Shutting the closet door behind her, Quinn shook her head. "Somehow, I think violin strings are too good for that witless creature." She snorted with derision.

Stomping over to her room, Quinn swung open the door. "Do you know what that fool cat did this–" Quinn's words were cut short by a sharp cry.

There, in front of her, sprawled face down on her bed lay Holly–stone still.

Three

Holly groaned and moved slightly at Quinn's cry. "Do you have to be so bloody loud?" she scolded from beneath a veil of wet blonde hair. "I'm trying to sleep here."

Quinn leaned weakly against the doorframe, afraid to move for fear her legs wouldn't hold her up. How many scares could a body take?

Holly pushed aside her wet tresses so she could peek at Quinn. "Are you all right, Quinn? You look like death."

Quinn pushed away from the doorway and closed the door behind her. "I'm not the only one," she muttered.

"What was that?" Holly asked, her voice muffled beneath her hair again.

"I just said, it's about time you're done."

Holly harrumphed. "It's not like you were waiting here eagerly. Where were you anyway?"

Quinn scooped up all she would need for her shower, including a change of clothing, and headed for the bathroom. "Just being entertained by Buttons."

"Buttons?" Holly pushed herself up onto her elbows. "That fried feline isn't in here again, is he?"

"No," Quinn answered from behind the bathroom

door. "I think that cat delights in giving people heart attacks."

"Aha!" Holly exclaimed. "That screwy cat got you, too, huh?"

Quinn undressed. "Yeah, and don't sound so happy about it either." Quinn could hear Holly giggling.

After a quick shower, Quinn dried her chin-length, dark, curly hair. She stared at her reflection in the mirror, making a face. She looked terrible. Maybe Miss Barrington wouldn't mind if they took a little nap, since there weren't any guests to attend to at the moment.

She opened the bathroom door and knew instantly that Holly had fallen asleep. The dead giveaway: she was snoring.

Quinn flopped down onto her bed, stretched out, and groaned as her body seemed to sigh with relief. She grabbed her little travel alarm, and she set it. An hour was more than a sufficient snooze.

The banging noise was really beginning to get on Quinn's nerves. She grabbed her pillow and squashed it over her head. Couldn't Dad fix stuff at a normal hour?

The banging continued. No, it was more like an insistent knock on a door. Quinn jolted completely awake and shoved herself into an upright position; her pillow fell to the floor.

The knock sounded again, bringing Quinn to her feet. She dashed past Holly, who was still sprawled across her bed fast asleep.

Quinn pulled the door open. "Miss Barrington," Quinn said, her voice breathless. "I'm sorry, but we were just–"

Edith held up her hand, cutting off Quinn's words. "I came to see if you girls were coming down for dinner."

"Dinner?" Quinn echoed stupidly. "Oh, yes, dinner. Of course." Quinn cleared her throat.

"We'll be right down. Thank you, Miss Barrington."

The older woman looked at her strangely before nodding and turning away. Quinn shut the door and leaned against it. Her heart pounded furiously from her sudden awakening. *I must have sounded like a total idiot.*

Pushing away from the door, she hurried to her small clock. She picked it up and tossed it with disgust back onto the night table. She'd set the alarm, but hadn't flicked up the alarm-on button.

"Holly, get up," Quinn called as she ran into the bathroom to comb her hair. Her clothes were a bit wrinkled, but they'd do. She came out of the bathroom. "Holly, get up," Quinn called louder. She grabbed and shook one of Holly's legs.

Holly moaned, kicking at the offending hand. "Bug off," she snarled irritably.

Quinn stood over Holly, her hands on her hips. "Get up, lazy. Miss Barrington was just here."

That got Holly's attention, she bolted upright. "Here? When?" She jumped off the bed and tore through her drawers for something to wear.

"Oh, about five minutes ago."

Holly looked appalled. "And you didn't wake me?"

Shaking her head with exasperation, Quinn plopped down on her bed to wait for Holly to dress. Holly's robe flew by her head, but she barely flinched, she simply watched her friend race around the room in a frenzy.

"Man, Quinn, how could you do this to me?" Holly asked as she emerged from the bathroom, pulling the last of her long blonde hair through a ponytail holder. "Miss Barrington probably thinks I'm lazy now."

Quinn cocked a dark brow at her friend. "If she thinks that about you, then she feels the same way about me, too."

"Good."

"Good?" Quinn echoed, giving Holly a *thanks-a-lot* look.

"Well, if I'm in trouble, I'd rather not be in it alone."

Quinn got off the bed and followed her to the door. "I doubt very much that either of us is in trouble. I'm sure they understand that it was a long flight here, then there's the time change, and we did clean the entire second floor."

Holly shut the door behind them. "I hope so. I'd hate to have to leave so soon."

As the girls made their way downstairs, Quinn couldn't help but remark, "Don't you find it odd that Miss Barrington is so concerned whether or not we eat?"

Holly smirked at Quinn. "Maybe she's trying to fatten us up so she and Eddie can cook us in that big black pot and eat us."

Holly laughed at her stupid joke, but some movement caught Quinn's eye. Edward Barrington was watching them from the front desk near the main entrance. Had he heard Holly's careless comment? He didn't smile or even acknowledge her, although they were staring right into each other's eyes. He must have heard. Quinn bit her lip as she broke eye contact.

"Let's get going, Hol. I'm starving."

They walked into the kitchen and stumbled upon Edith at the big black pot. She quickly closed the lid as the girls came in.

"Are all the rooms on the second floor cleaned?" she asked as she came around the counter to meet them.

"Yes," Holly piped up. "But we were wondering why–"

"Good, good," Edith interrupted as she guided them to the small kitchen table. "Three guests have arrived."

Holly and Quinn looked at each other and winced as they sat down. Maybe that was why Edward Barrington looked so annoyed, Quinn thought worriedly. Not even here a day and already they were slackers.

"I hope roast beef, mashed potatoes and gravy, and mixed vegetables are all right," Edith asked as she filled two plates. It wasn't really a question, more a statement.

She set their plates in front of them, along with two cups and a pot of tea. Quinn prayed Holly wouldn't say anything about not liking tea. They were probably in enough trouble already. From the dining room, they could hear the clanging of cutlery and the tinkling of glass. To make matters worse, they overheard Edward Barrington say that the guests' rooms were ready, and that he would take their bags upstairs.

After they quickly gobbled down their meal, they offered to help Edith, who'd begun to clear away the dining room dishes.

Edith glanced up from the table she'd started. "That would be nice," she said without smiling. Without another word, she went back into the kitchen.

"Maybe we should just pack our bags," Holly said mournfully as she cleaned one of the two tables used.

Quinn worked on the other, not replying. She hoped the Barringtons weren't too upset with them.

The moment they were done in the dining room, Edith separated them. She sent Quinn to relieve Mr. Barrington at the front desk, and kept Holly to help with the dishes.

Mr. Barrington left without a word just as three more guests arrived–a man, a woman, and a young man–a very cute young man.

"Can I help you?" Quinn asked, putting on her best smile.

The older man dropped the suitcases he was carrying onto the floor with a bang and exhaled harshly as he straightened. "We're the Caines; we have a reservation."

Quinn glanced at the young man who stood by silently; holding two other suitcases that looked even heavier than the ones the older gentleman had been carrying. Then she quickly flipped through the pages of the guest register.

"Yes," she said as she found their name. "You'll be in Rooms 10 and 11." She stood up and placed the book on the small counter, just above the desk. "Would you sign in, please?"

As the elder Caine signed the register, she reached for the appropriate keys. She handed them to Mr. Caine, then cast another glance at the man's very tall, very handsome, dark-haired son.

"Thank you," the older man said, picking up the

suitcases again.

"If you like, I'll show you to your rooms?" Quinn offered, and was rewarded with a devastating smile from the son. She swallowed, her heart skipping a beat.

"That would be wonderful," Mrs. Caine finally spoke up.

"Follow me." Quinn motioned them with her hand then led them up the marble staircase, turned right, and went all the way down the hall, stopping just short of the room she and Holly shared, Room 12.

"Here you are," Quinn chirped. "If there's anything else you need, just ask. My name is Quinn Hunter." She tried to say this to Mr. and Mrs. Caine, but her gaze was drawn to their son.

"Thank you, Quinn," Mr. Caine said as he went into Room 11, followed by his wife. They shut the door softly behind them.

"I guess I get Room 10," the younger Caine said, breaking the silence that had fallen over them. His voice, deep and smooth, drizzled over Quinn like warm honey.

"I guess," she returned, and then bristled at how stupid she sounded.

"My name is Jaxon Caine, but you can call me Jax, all my friends do." He smiled at her again, and the light in his green eyes danced mischievously.

She felt herself smiling back. "A pleasure, Jax. And I'm–"

"Quinn," he supplied.

She blushed. "Right, I already told you that, didn't I?" She glanced around the empty hall, feeling foolish.

"Well, I better get inside," he said, trying to catch her

gaze with his.

Quinn smiled self-consciously. "Yeah." She started to walk away.

"Will I see you around?" he asked, forcing her to stop and turn around.

"Sure, my room is just over there," she said, pointing to Room 12, the room next to his. She blushed again.

What the heck was she doing, telling a strange boy where her room was? He probably thinks I'm a total freak, Quinn thought irritably. Or worse, that I'm inviting him over for who knows what.

His lips pulled back in another smile, showing a set of even, white teeth. "Later, Quinn." He disappeared into his room.

For a moment, she just stood there, feeling like she'd just made a complete and total fool of herself. She threw up her hands. What did it matter anyway? Once he got a look at Holly he'd forget she existed. With a sigh, she returned to the front desk, only to find Holly lounging carelessly in a chair behind the desk.

"You all done helping Miss Barrington in the kitchen?" Quinn asked as she pulled up another chair.

Holly leaned back as far as she could on her chair and stretched, making a lot of groaning noises in the process. "Yeah, finally." She straightened. "She said to help you around here a little. You know, to get the feel of things." She rolled her eyes. "You been busy?"

"A little. Mostly tidying and stuff."

"I heard there's new guests," Holly commented off-handedly.

Quinn glanced at her. "And how would you know

that?"

"Is he as cute up close?" Holly demanded eagerly.

"You were hiding and watching, weren't you?"

"Well, is he?" Holly asked again, not denying anything.

Quinn shook her head and sighed. "He's better."

Holly laughed out loud and spun her chair in a circle. "What's his name?" she asked, suddenly halting her spin.

Quinn chewed on the inside of her cheek. She knew this would happen. But guys come and go, and Holly was her best friend. Holly was here to stay.

"Jaxon Caine," she supplied, then went to a beige filing cabinet, and began rummaging through it. The files were mixed up. She pulled some out and began to alphabetize them.

Holly stayed quiet for a moment, then asked, "Why do you suppose the rooms on the second floor were so dirty, Quinn?"

Quinn stopped what she was doing, shocked–no, stunned that Holly had changed the subject. Besides mystery books, guys were Holly's favorite subject.

"I don't know," Quinn admitted. She went over to stand beside Holly's chair. "But I'll tell you something even stranger. While you were in the shower earlier, I heard a weird scraping noise. It was coming from the third floor." Quinn sat down on the edge of the desk. "You know that narrow little door that's right across from ours?"

"The little closet?"

Quinn shook her head. "It's more than that. Inside was a flight of stairs hidden behind a door at the back of the closet."

"Stairs? In a closet?" Holly shook her head. "How did you know to look there?"

"I didn't. The door was ajar, and I'm just naturally nosy." Quinn grinned.

Holly cocked her blonde eyebrows. "This is beginning to sound like a mystery novel."

Quinn shot her a wry look. "Please, let's not get carried away."

"But it sounds like a secret passageway."

"So?"

Holly made a face. "So, nothing. I just think it's cool. I'll bet this old place has dozens of creepy secret passageways."

"Can I continue?" Quinn demanded dryly.

Holly snorted, sitting back in her chair. "Be my guest." She waved her hand.

"Thank you. Anyway, I used the stairs and they lead up to the third floor. It was spotless up there, Holly."

"Spotless?"

Quinn nodded. "Yeah. Clean as a whistle."

Holly frowned. "Man, that is strange."

Quinn snorted. "You said it. And I just realized something else."

"What?"

"Other than the stairway in that closet, I don't remember seeing any other staircase leading to the third floor, do you?"

Holly thought about it for a moment. "No, and we cleaned the entire second floor."

Quinn shook her head slowly in confusion. "It just

doesn't make sense. Why would anyone want to hide the staircase to the third floor? And why bother keeping it clean when the second floor, the one in use, is so untidy?" Quinn puzzled over her thoughts.

Suddenly, Holly suddenly jumped up and screamed.

Four

Quinn nearly leaped out of her skin. "What the devil is wrong with you," she demanded.

But Holly didn't answer. She hurried over to an old picture of a woman and stared at it. "Did you see her eyes move?"

Quinn stared at her friend in amazement. "What?"

Holly looked over her shoulder, her face in a panic. "Her *eyes*. Did you see them move?"

Quinn got up and went over to the painting. She looked at the picture. It looked fine to her. "Are you trying to scare me?" Quinn asked suspiciously.

"Scare you?" Holly stared into Quinn's eyes for a moment, saying nothing then, "You really didn't see anything?"

Quinn shook her head slowly.

Holly grabbed her head in her hands and moaned.

"Are you girls all right?" Edward Barrington asked from behind them. They spun around. "I thought I heard someone scream."

Holly's eyes caught and held Quinn's, looking desperate.

"Holly just saw a spider, Mr. Barrington," Quinn supplied, thinking quickly.

He looked at them suspiciously. "Are you sure?"

Holly nodded. "It was a real big one. Ugly and creepy looking." She shivered for effect.

This time Quinn felt like groaning. "I'm sorry we disturbed you, Mr. Barrington."

His pale blue eyes studied them. "Well, if you're sure everything's all right."

"Everything's fine," Quinn said quickly. The girls stood side by side with stupid smiles pasted on their faces until he left, then Quinn turned on her friend. "Are you crazy!"

Holly looked at the picture again. "I really thought I saw the eyes in the picture move."

"Hol, it was probably just a play of light. I'm sure..."

Behind the wall, a darkly cloaked figure listened to the girls arguing, their voices muffled by the plasterboard. The figure's breathing rasped in the stillness as a covered limb rose to slide back the panel behind the eyes of the picture. The figure watched, and its breath quickened at the sight of the girls.

"So, pretty...so pretty..."

Drool trickled from the figure's lips, ran unchecked down its chin, and disappeared beneath the dark cloak.

"Pretty," the figure chanted softly, "so pretty..."

"Do you realize how crazy that sounds?" Quinn insisted.

The girls sorted through the files, placing them in alphabetical order as they argued.

"If you had just looked when I told you to, maybe

you would have seen it, too." With a file in each hand, Holly waved her arms about, looking like she was ready to take flight. She motioned toward the picture with both files, and then halted her tirade. "You see! They moved again!" She dropped the files and bolted over to the picture.

Quinn didn't move, merely glanced at the picture. "Right, Hol, I think perhaps someone might need glasses."

The eyes of the picture stayed perfectly still as Holly squinted at them. "I do not," she complained. "I see this picture just fine." Holly couldn't get her face any closer without squashing her nose against it.

"Fine is not the word *I* would use."

Holly spun around and stomped back to the filing cabinet. "Oh, really. And just what word would *you* use, O Great One?"

"Excuse me, ladies," a deep voice interrupted.

Quinn recognized Jaxon Caine immediately, and blushed at being caught in such an embarrassing situation.

"Do you happen to know what people do for entertainment around here?" He smiled at them.

Quinn's heart jumped in her chest, and one look at Holly said that Jaxon had the same effect on her.

Holly flashed her most brilliant smile. A thousand-watt smile, for sure. "You must be Jaxon Caine. Quinn told me all about you."

He cocked a dark brow at Quinn, who blushed again. "I don't believe I've had the pleasure," he said, glancing back at Holly.

"Holly Gates," she said as she edged closer to the desk with her hand outstretched.

Jaxon shook it, then stuffed his hands into the pockets of his tan pants. "So, do you know where the action is?"

Quinn finally found her voice. "Actually, we just arrived on Maui this morning." She shrugged. "I'm afraid we don't know any more about this place than you do. Sorry."

"*Hmm*," he murmured, cupping his cute, dimpled chin in his hand. "I don't suppose you ladies would be interested in exploring what this island has to offer, would you?"

Holly and Quinn glanced at each other, and then Quinn said, "I don't–"

"We'd love to," Holly interrupted. "But we don't get off until eight tonight."

Jaxon glanced at his watch. "All right. I'll be back in a half hour."

Holly's lips curved into a huge smile. "Could you make it eight-fifteen? We need to freshen up."

His mouth turned up at the corners. "Eight-fifteen it is."

"Perfect," Holly returned.

"Later then," he said, turning away with a wave.

"Just what the devil are you doing?" Quinn whispered harshly. "Miss Barrington didn't say when we get off."

Holly watched Jaxon until he was out of sight before looking back at Quinn. "Actually, she did."

Quinn shook her head with exasperation. "What are you talking about?"

"When I was helping Edith in the kitchen, she told me we could call it a night at eight."

"Edith?" Quinn questioned. "That's pretty familiar."

Holly made a face. "We're the best of friends, now. I'm thinking of trading you in."

"You wouldn't last three minutes without me."

Holly snorted.

"Did 'your best friend' tell you anything else?" Quinn asked. "Like our schedule? As much as I enjoy working with you, Miss Barrington did mention separating us."

"The horror," Holly cried, tipping her head back and placing the back of her hand against her brow like a movie star from an old black-and-white movie.

Quinn shook her head as she went back to the files. "Over-actor."

Holly just laughed, following Quinn. "Let's see," Holly began, as she picked up a few files. "You start at nine in the morning till six on desk duty, with a one-hour lunch break. Mr. Barrington will relieve you and watch the desk in the evening. While I," she cocked her head with a *lucky me* look, "get the pleasure of kitchen, housekeeping, and laundry duties. But at least I don't have to cook, Miss Barrington takes care of that." Holly smiled mischievously. "I do get to sleep in, though."

Quinn glanced at her questioningly. "What do you mean?"

"I don't start until ten. This place has buffet breakfasts, so I don't have to serve in the morning, just clean up."

Quinn cocked her brow. "And what if there are a lot of guests and not enough tables? Who clears them till you get your sorry butt to work?"

Their gazes locked, then Holly said, "Even if there

were a lot of guests–and I doubt it–Miss Barrington clears the dishes and stacks them by the dishwasher."

"And when do I get my turn to enjoy eight glorious hours of cleaning?" Quinn asked, not too eager about the prospect.

"We switch Sundays."

"Wonderful," Quinn returned dryly.

"Well, you can't do the fun job all the time, Quinn."

Quinn rolled her eyes. "Oh, yeah, this is *sooo* much fun." She waved a file for emphasis.

Holly stuffed a file into the cabinet and slammed the drawer shut. "Save those for tomorrow," she suggested, nodding toward the stack of files on the desk. "It's time to rock and roll."

Quinn didn't feel like going out, but Holly had promised. Quinn dropped the file she was holding onto the pile and followed Holly up to their room.

They changed, applied fresh make-up, and restyled their hair. They had just finished when there was a knock at the door.

Quinn tossed a look at Holly. "Are you sure it was okay to leave the reception desk?"

Holly headed for the door. "Yes, I'm sure," she returned in a mocking voice. She opened the door, making a little squeak of surprise at who was there.

"I hope I'm not too early," Jaxon said. He glanced past Holly, his green-eyed gaze resting on Quinn.

Holly shook herself out of her stupor. "Ah, no. We're ready. But how did you–"

"I told him," Quinn cut in, coming up behind Holly.

Holly gave her a raised-eyebrow look, but said

nothing.

"I thought we'd go to Lahaina," Jaxon suggested. He stepped aside to let them pass, then followed them downstairs.

The warm air hit them hard as they left the air-conditioned comfort of Barrington House, but the gently blowing trade winds soon cooled things off. He took them to a brand new Pontiac Sunfire and opened the front door. Holly slipped into the front seat, tossing her long blonde hair over her shoulder as she reached for the seatbelt. Jaxon closed the door and gave Quinn an apologetic look.

He walked around to the other side, opened the door, moved the seat ahead, and let Quinn into the back. Quinn just smiled. She was used to taking the back seat, in more ways than one.

The sky was dark as they zipped along the highway toward Lahaina. Jaxon found a local rock station on the radio and turned up the volume.

Quinn silently mouthed the words to a familiar song, while the wind rushed through the open window and tousled her hair.

When they arrived at Lahaina, they explored the streets a little before pulling into a parking lot on the corner of Front and Prison Street. A car backed out of a slot.

"Wow, that was lucky," Jax said as he pulled into the vacant space. "Parking is crazy around here."

He cut the engine of the Sunfire and leaned over Holly to open the glove compartment. He pulled out a book.

"A travel guide." Holly smirked at Quinn. "What a great idea."

Jaxon checked the index and thumbed to the section that read, *Where to Stay - What to See - Lahaina.*

"What do you think of the Hard Rock Cafe?" he asked, glancing first at Holly, then at Quinn.

"I'm game," Holly piped up. "This is going to be fun!"

"I'm sure it'll be great," Quinn returned, her voice flat. Quinn wasn't really hungry, but she didn't want to be a drag. "I guess a movie is out of the question."

Jaxon opened his door and climbed out. The girls followed suit.

"We've already decided on the Hard Rock Cafe, Quinn," Holly said airily, straightening her short black skirt.

"Right," Quinn muttered with a sigh.

Holly, Quinn, and Jaxon headed down Front Street.

"I hope you don't mind walking. Parking is limited."

Holly threaded her arm through Jaxon's and held it tightly. "Nope. It's a beautiful night for a walk."

Quinn rolled her eyes. Sometimes Holly could be so obvious.

Jaxon glanced over his shoulder at Quinn. "Hey, stranger, lonely back there?"

Quinn smiled. "Not at all. The view is too beautiful."

"Really?" He grinned devilishly at her, and she turned red.

"I didn't mean–"

"Isn't that a darling outfit, Quinn?" Holly cut in.

Quinn looked at the outfit displayed in a storefront window. "Yeah, it's great," Quinn returned sullenly. Silently, she thanked Holly for keeping her from sticking her foot into her mouth, yet again. Quinn swore to keep her mouth shut.

She turned her attention to the sights around her, feeling like she'd stepped back in time. The street lamps bathed the buildings with a soft light, giving the colorful structures an ambiance of warmth. Definitely not the same feeling Barrington House had given her. Quinn smiled. She wanted to reach out and hold onto the feeling forever.

"Hey, Quinn. Where ya going?" Holly asked. She and Jaxon had stopped in front of an entrance.

Quinn stopped, blinked, and glanced around. A strand of dark hair blew forward and tickled her nose. She brushed it aside.

"Wow, Quinn," Holly teased. "You in the Twilight Zone or what?"

Quinn squeezed her eyes shut at the wave of humiliation. Was she always going to make a fool of herself in front of Jax? She slowly turned around. "Sorry, too caught up in the sights."

"I know what you mean," Jaxon agreed. He untangled himself from Holly. "I've traveled a bit, and I have to tell you, this place is by far the most beautiful."

Quinn swallowed hard, her heart pounding. She stared at Jax. There was a strange light in his eyes. Could he have meant *her*? That she was beautiful?

He turned back to Holly and laughed at something she'd said.

Nah, get serious, Quinn scolded herself. It's not you he thinks is pretty.

Quinn could hear rock music coming from the Hard Rock Cafe, right out into the street. How could she have missed it? She shrugged, following the other two inside.

She looked around, wide-eyed. The place was great. It was dimly lit and crowded. It had a '60s decor with guitars, big surfboards, concert posters, and music memorabilia decorating the walls and surrounding areas. There was even a Cadillac over the bar.

Bar!

"Isn't this great?" Holly said in Quinn's ear.

"Yeah, yeah, great," Quinn replied absently. She tapped Jaxon on the arm. "We're not twenty-one."

Jaxon smiled. "Neither am I, but this is a cafe, remember? We can eat here as long as we don't drink."

"Not even cola?" Holly cracked.

"I think they can manage that," Jaxon returned, grinning at Holly.

"A table for three?" the hostess asked, smiling politely.

"Yeah," Jaxon answered.

"This way, please."

They followed the young woman to a table away from the crowd. Jaxon chose to sit beside Quinn, which surprised her. She felt warm and giddy inside, and tried not to notice Holly's frown.

The hostess placed menus in front of them. "Your waitress will be with you shortly."

They'd barely had time to glance at the menus when the waitress arrived. "My name is Jodi, and I'll be your waitress this evening. Can I get you anything to drink while you decide on your order?" she asked, all the while watching them carefully.

"Not right now. We'll order our sodas with our meal," Jaxon replied, and Quinn noticed the woman visibly relax.

"I'll be back shortly," the waitress said, and disappeared into the crowd.

"I think we passed," Quinn ventured.

"Passed what?" Holly asked as she scanned her menu.

Quinn glanced at her menu as well. "That waitress was testing us."

Holly glanced up. "For what?"

"To see if we'd order any alcohol," Quinn informed her. "She knew we were underage."

Holly turned her gaze to Jaxon, who nodded. "I didn't even notice," she said.

Quinn smiled as she turned back to her menu. For once she wasn't the one to take a short brain vacation.

The waitress reappeared a few minutes later. "You folks ready to order?"

"I think I'll have the barbecued lime chicken with baked potato, and salad," Holly ordered then laid her menu in front of the waitress.

"Anything to drink?" she asked.

"Diet cola, please."

The waitress quickly scribbled down Holly's order, then turned to Quinn.

Quinn glanced at Holly, wondering how she could order such a large meal after having supper earlier. She cleared her throat. "I'll just have a salad with the house dressing, and a regular cola."

"And I'll have the barbecued ribs, french fries, and mixed vegetables. And could I get a regular cola, as well?" Jax asked.

The waitress finished the order and tucked her pencil behind her ear. "It'll be about thirty minutes; it's a little busy tonight," she told them as she scooped up the menus. "I'll bring your drinks while you wait."

Quinn glanced around the room, quietly enjoying herself. Earlier, she hadn't wanted to come, but now she was glad she had. She peeked at Jaxon as he talked with Holly. Why had he chosen to sit next to her and not Holly?

She tried to shake off the excited feeling. *Don't see more into it than there is*, she scolded silently. He was probably just being nice.

The smell of teriyaki filled her nostrils and made her stomach grumble. She winced; maybe she was hungrier than she thought.

The waitress came with their drinks, and Quinn took a sip of the icy liquid. It tingled as it slid down her throat. As she took another swallow, she began to choke as her eyes connected with a cold pair of blue ones.

A very familiar pair.

Five

Jaxon pounded on Quinn's back as Holly came around the table, her pretty face concerned.

"Are you all right?" she asked.

"Mr.–" Quinn went into another coughing fit. When she got herself under control, she tried again. "Mr. Barrington," she rasped. "He's here."

"What?" Holly exclaimed, straightening immediately.

Quinn wiped her eyes and tried to clear her throat. "I saw Mr. Barrington."

"Here?" Holly demanded as she looked around, scanning every face.

Quinn cleared her throat yet again. "Over there," she said, pointing toward the bar.

Holly stared hard at the people crowded at the bar. "I seem to recall someone saying that *I* needed glasses," Holly commented, her hands on her hips.

Quinn dismissed the joke. "I saw him, Hol," she insisted, a little desperately. "Right there, by the bar. He was staring at us. He looked really mad."

With a swing of her blonde mane, Holly reclaimed her seat. "It wasn't Edward Barrington."

"I swear it was," Quinn exclaimed. She lowered her voice. "Are you sure it was okay for us to leave at eight?"

Holly cocked her head, her face filled with annoyance. "Miss Barrington said we could go. If there's been some kind of misunderstanding, it's not our problem."

"Is everything all right?" Jaxon finally spoke up. He looked warily from one face to the other. "You didn't skip out on your jobs, did you?"

Holly let out an exasperated sigh. "Edith Barrington said that we could leave at eight o'clock. Now what part of that didn't either of you understand?"

Holly took a long swig of her diet cola, then looked around and bobbed her head to the music.

She's angry, Quinn realized. And why shouldn't she be? Quinn had questioned her about something private in front of Jax. And Holly didn't lie. If Miss Barrington said they could leave at eight o'clock, then that's what she said.

"Look, Hol," Quinn began. "I'm sorry I doubted you."

Holly waved the words away and didn't reply. Quinn sighed.

She glanced around the cafe. She was sure it had been Edward Barrington, and he'd looked so angry.

But where was he now? Had she imagined him?

The questions rolled around in Quinn's head. She'd had a strange feeling since she'd arrived at Barrington House, and for just a little while that feeling had faded. Maybe her subconscious was just trying to keep her alert— force her to remember not to let her guard down.

"There she goes again."

Quinn glanced at Holly, who shook her head at Quinn.

"Visiting Mars, are we?" Holly remarked, blonde brows cocked over blue eyes. She picked up her fork and dug into her baked potato. It was already smeared with butter, sour cream, and bacon bits.

Their meal had arrived and Quinn hadn't even noticed. She sighed again and picked up the little plastic cup filled with salad dressing. She glanced at Jaxon as she poured it over the salad; he was silent as he picked at his meal.

I bet he'll be glad when this evening is over, Quinn mused unhappily.

No one spoke on the ride back to Barrington House, and Jaxon only gave them a polite "Goodnight" before disappearing into his room.

"I blew the evening, didn't I?" Quinn questioned as she changed into a long T-shirt nightgown with the saying, *I refuse to rise and shine.*

Holly snorted as she brushed her long hair, her face hidden beneath its veil.

"I really am sorry about doubting you, Hol." Quinn went to sit beside her friend on her bed. "Especially in front of Jaxon."

Holly flipped her head back, her hair flying like a golden banner. She stared at Quinn. "I think Jaxon likes you, Quinn."

This time Quinn snorted. "Yeah, right." She got off Holly's bed and went into the bathroom, leaving the door open. She grabbed her toothbrush, squeezed on some toothpaste, then shoved it into her mouth.

Holly came up behind Quinn, watching her in the mirror as she scrubbed her teeth roughly. "Really, I think the guy has got it bad for you."

"With you around, Hol?" Quinn returned, her mouth full of toothpaste.

Holly sighed, and Quinn felt terrible about her words. She spat out the toothpaste and rinsed her mouth, then turned to her friend. "That was uncalled for. I'm sorry."

"It's all right," Holly said softly. She fingered a white hand-towel that hung on the rack beside the bathroom counter. "I can be a real snot sometimes."

Quinn frowned. "That's not true. You just like guys, that's all."

"How many guys have I taken from you?"

Quinn was stunned by Holly's words. Holly looked so serious, so vulnerable, so...un-Holly-like. "None worth mentioning."

Holly stared deeply into Quinn's eyes then turned and silently left the bathroom. Quinn watched her go. After washing her face, she returned to the bedroom.

Holly tried to scoot into the bathroom, but hesitated when Quinn called her name. "No guy is worth our friendship, Hol. In a few days, Jaxon will be gone." Quinn shrugged. "Guys come and go, but we'll always be friends."

Holly glanced over her shoulder at Quinn and smiled a crooked smile. "You'll make a good shrink someday, Quinn."

"You just remember me when you're a national best-selling author."

"Why? Do you think I'll need your help?" Holly quipped.

Quinn looked thoughtful. "Well, you do plan to write

mystery, and it would be extremely interesting to find out where you get your weird ideas."

Holly tapped her finger to her head. "From the dark recesses of my twisted mind."

"That's what I was afraid of," Quinn returned with a shake of her head. "If I had a business card, I'd give you one right now and tell you to call me."

Holly waved Quinn's words away as she disappeared into the bathroom. "I already know your number."

Quinn chuckled as she crawled into bed. She snuggled beneath a thin sheet and closed her eyes. Over the soft hum of the air conditioner, she heard Holly creep around the room for a few minutes, before turning off the light and slipping into her own bed.

Quinn was so tired she thought she would drift off to sleep quickly, but she didn't. After a short time, she could hear Holly's even breathing, signaling that her friend had fallen asleep.

Slipping out of bed, she quietly tiptoed to the balcony doors and went out into the night, closing the glass door soundlessly behind her. Standing at the railing, she rested her hands on the warm metal. She expelled a soft breath, letting the trade winds caress her face.

The dark sky was filled with dancing starlight, and sweet smells from the garden below tickled her senses. She could hear the water gently lap against the shore; and far in the distance, the faint sounds of music. Someone must be having a beach party, she mused.

The ocean sparkled in the moonlight like a huge jewel, drawing her gaze. She and Holly would have to hit the beach on their first day off.

Suddenly, a strange sensation sent prickles up and down her spine. She tensed.

Someone was watching her!

She glanced back into her room. Holly was still sleeping, her back to Quinn. Quinn squinted into the night. Was someone down in the garden? She watched for movement. Then her hair stood up on the back of her neck.

She stiffened, turning her eyes upward, toward the third floor, but she was unable to see the windows clearly. Without thinking, she leaned dangerously over the railing; and peered up at the third floor.

In the window, was that a silhouette?

Quinn gasped. She couldn't make out any features; everything was dark about the person.

She began to tremble despite the warm night. Who was that...Edward Barrington? A wave of dizziness washed over her as the world shifted and moved before her eyes, and for a moment, she felt weightless.

Reality checked in instantly as she tumbled backwards over the railing. A scream caught in her throat as she frantically grabbed hold of one of the thin bars supporting the railing. Her wrist twisted unmercifully and she slammed her chest into the balcony's thick wooden base. Pain exploded through her, nearly causing her to lose her handhold. With all her weight pulling heavily on one arm, it felt like it was being ripped from its socket.

Dangling precariously, she reached up to grasp another thin bar. She gripped it hard then whimpered as her fear-dampened hands slowly slid down the black metal to the base.

How was she going to get back up? A sob tore at her throat, making it burn.

"Holly," she tried to call out. Her breathing came in short gasps, and tears coursed down her face.

Holly couldn't hear her. Not through the thick glass of the balcony doors. Not with the air conditioner running.

Quinn choked back another sob. Her hands were slipping. She readjusted her hands, tightly grasping the slick metal. Her arms burned beneath her weight. Her chest throbbed and her head was spinning.

She was going to fall!

She was going to plunge to the hard cobblestone patio below, and she would lay there, her body broken and bloody, and no one would even know until tomorrow. She shivered, and her hands slid again. Quinn gasped, sobbing.

Suddenly, the balcony doors banged open. Someone stepped out onto the balcony and peered over the edge. Quinn craned her neck, looking up.

Oh my God! It was the person from the third floor!

Six

"*Quinn*," a male voice called.

A second person suddenly leaned over the balcony.

"Oh, my God," a girl's voice cried.

"I'm going to reach down and grab your hands."

Jax? Quinn started to cry.

"It's all right," Jaxon assured her as he leaned over the railing and took hold of her wrists. "Hold my legs, Holly," he ordered.

His fingers moved over Quinn's wrists until he felt he had a good grip, and then he pulled.

"Let go!" he commanded, jerking her hands to release them.

"I can't," Quinn cried. "My fingers won't move."

"Pry her fingers away from the bars," he barked at Holly.

Holly crouched down and pulled at Quinn's fingers. A searing pain shot up Quinn's arms, but she miraculously kept from crying out. Quinn's full weight jerked Jaxon forward, slamming his chest against the railing. He grunted in pain.

"Hold onto me, Holly," he ordered through gritted teeth.

Together, they tugged and pulled at Quinn, bringing

her up and over the railing onto the hard, cool wood of the balcony floor, taking Jaxon and Holly with her. All three of them lay there, entangled with each other, panting hard.

"Damn it, Quinn!" Holly swore, pushing herself up into a sitting position. "You could have broken your neck."

Quinn lay on her back, still breathing hard. "Thanks for enlightening me on that fact, Hol."

Holly shifted position. "What the heck happened?" she demanded.

Quinn felt extremely dumb. "I saw someone. Up there, on the third floor." She pointed to the window where she'd seen the person who'd been watching her. No one was there now. *Figures.*

"Are you sure this wasn't just another sighting? Like seeing Edward Barrington at the Hard Rock Cafe?" Holly inquired.

Quinn pushed her aching body up into a sitting position, too. "I *saw* someone up there, Holly. He was watching me."

"So, how the heck did you fall over the railing?" Holly demanded, getting up and standing over her.

Quinn thought Holly looked like an angry kindergarten teacher, with her stern look and her hands on her hips.

"It was an accident," Quinn began, painfully trying to get up. Jaxon stood up and helped her to her feet. She thanked him quietly, not looking him in the eyes. "I was leaning backward over the railing, trying to get a better look at the person spying on me." Quinn shrugged. "I guess I just leaned back a little too far."

"Obviously," Holly put in sarcastically.

Everyone fell silent for a moment, and then Quinn asked Holly, "How did you know? I mean, I called out, but I was sure no one heard me."

"I didn't hear you. It was Jaxon," Holly said. "If he hadn't been out on his balcony and seen you fall over, you'd still be hanging there!"

Holly stormed back into the room, leaving Quinn alone with Jaxon, who thus far hadn't said a word.

"She's right, you know," Jaxon said quietly. "I couldn't sleep, so I went out onto the balcony. I thought I was alone, until I looked over here and saw you go over the edge."

Over the edge is right, Quinn grumbled silently, *in more ways than one.*

"Thank you for saving me," Quinn said, watching his face carefully. It was blank.

He doesn't like me, Quinn mused unhappily. *Especially since I ruined the evening. And now, this...* She wanted to groan her frustration.

He moved over to the edge of the balcony and looked out at the ocean. For a long time he said nothing. Finally, "A year ago, I lost a friend," he said quietly, "at a party. My friend's parents weren't home and we were all drinking." He glanced at Quinn. "We were so stupid, sneaking around, stealing the booze from her parents. She got so wasted, and she thought it would be a real hoot to walk the edge of the balcony railing. She lived on the 12th floor." He swallowed hard and stared down at his fingers gripping the railing. "Needless to say, she didn't make it."

Quinn shivered.

"She was a talented pianist," he went on, "and she had a wonderful future. It was such a waste."

Quinn touched his arm. "I'm sorry."

He put his hand over hers and gazed into her eyes. With his other hand, he touched her cheek, stroking his thumb along her jawbone. "I'm just glad you're okay."

She trembled and held her breath. Jax leaned closer, hesitantly, then closer still, gently touching his lips to hers. Quinn's eyes slid shut, and a feeling of intense warmth spread through her limbs.

He pulled away, leaned his forehead against hers, then said, "I should be going." He drew away from her, leaving her feeling chilled. "Do you think you'll be all right now?"

Quinn couldn't trust herself to talk, so she simply nodded. He stared at her for a moment longer, before disappearing into her room.

For a moment, Quinn just stood there. What had just happened? She touched her lips. With a sigh, she too, went inside.

Shutting the glass doors, she locked them and went to bed. She glanced at Holly, who was sleeping. Holly had been ticked, and with good reason; she'd been given quite a scare. Quinn could only imagine what she looked like hanging off the balcony.

A great tiredness washed over Quinn as she stole a quick peek at her clock. It was late, really late, and she had to get up early.

Pushing all thoughts from her mind, she snuggled deeply beneath the sheet. She was so tired. Within a few minutes, she drifted off.

The bedroom door creaked open slowly, allowing the light from the hallway to shine into the room. Ragged breathing softly filled the silence.

The white light spilled over the pretty face of the blonde-haired girl. She flinched, moaned, and rolled over, before lying still again. The figure's head turned slightly, to take in the sleeping form of the other girl, the dark-haired one.

So pretty. Both of them...so pretty.

A desperate wanting seemed to radiate from the dark form as its eyes lovingly caressed the dark-haired girl's face. Its heart quickened and its breathing got even harsher.

Stepping forward, the figure released its tight grip on the door handle, and the handle spun loudly back into position.

The dark-haired girl gasped, sitting up. "Who's there?" she called.

But the shadowy figure was gone.

Quinn stared hard at the open door, her heart pounding, and the light, bright to her eyes.

"Who's there?" she called again.

Crawling painfully out of bed, she went to the door and cautiously glanced out. Then creeping out further, she checked the hall, first one way, and then the other.

With a sigh, she closed the door and fumbled to lock it. Jaxon must have forgotten to close the door all the way. It must have opened on its own.

Quinn went back to bed. Her heart was still throbbing wildly, and it was a long while before she calmed down enough to fall asleep again.

The morning light spilled in through the parted curtains. Quinn moaned, annoyed that she'd left them open last night. Her alarm went off and she bolted upright.

Man, she hated clocks.

She groaned as she lay down again. Her body was a million aching parts. This bed sure is crappy, she mused, rubbing her ribs. Then it hit her.

The balcony…hanging from it by her fingertips. It hadn't been a dream.

She tested her aching arms, the muscles protesting each movement. Her fingers were curled and tight. She tried to straighten them and flinched, biting her lip at the white-hot pain.

She glanced at the clock again; seven-fifty a.m. She had to get moving. She started work at nine.

Quinn peeked at Holly, who was snoring softly, her hand tucked beneath her blonde head.

At least she gets to sleep in, Quinn grumbled silently, pushing her battered body out of bed. She stumbled toward the bathroom, shutting the door quietly behind her. It took a few moments of fumbling, but she finally got her hands to work well enough to turn on the shower. Stepping beneath the hot spray of water, she let it work its magic, loosening all her aching muscles, especially the ones in her hands.

By the time she'd dried off, her hands were less stiff,

and her fingers moved with only minor discomfort. Thank goodness, she thought. She'd have been totally useless today. *You still might be*, a voice niggled at the back of her mind.

After drying her hair and getting dressed, she slipped out of the room and made her way to the kitchen, not even glancing at Jaxon's room as she passed it.

"Good morning, Miss Barrington," Quinn greeted then helped herself to a bowl of porridge.

"Good morning, Quinn," Miss Barrington returned. "Sleep well?"

"Ah, just great," she lied. She sat down, sprinkled some brown sugar on her cereal, then added milk.

"Did you do anything interesting last night?" asked Miss Barrington.

Quinn nearly spat out her porridge. If you call thinking she'd seen Edward Barrington at the Hard Rock Cafe, hanging off a balcony like Spiderman, and kissing Jaxon Caine interesting? Then yes, she'd have to say she'd had a *very* interesting night.

"No, just the usual," she said instead.

"How did you find the reception desk yesterday?"

"Fine."

The older lady sat across from Quinn. "No problems with the switchboard? I'm sorry, I should have taken a moment to show you how it works."

"That's all right," Quinn said. "No one called."

"Do you think there will be any problems?" the woman persisted. "I can give you a quick lesson?"

Quinn shook her head. "I think I'll be all right. I took a look at it during a quiet spell. It doesn't look too difficult to figure out."

Edith made a sharp nodding motion with her head. "Good." She got up and returned to her work.

Feeling dismissed, Quinn placed her empty bowl near the sink, then went to the fridge, grabbed a can of diet cola, and left the kitchen. She'd just gotten comfortable at the front desk when the phone rang.

A couple of hours later, Quinn had taken a half-dozen calls, checked in a couple, and checked out one guest, before she'd had a break. Her head was spinning. Just then, Holly came down the stairs in a bikini and a wrap.

"Um, what are you doing?" Quinn asked, giving her friend a confused look.

Holly flounced over to the desk. "I am going to the beach with Jaxon."

"When you were outlining our duties the other day, I don't remember there being anything about going to the beach in the middle of the shift," Quinn commented dryly.

Holly smiled. "I ran out of work," she said with a shrug. "So, I'm taking my lunch break early. One beautiful hour to kill." She glanced at the staircase just as Jaxon made his way down. She grinned devilishly at Quinn. "And what a way to go."

"Mornin', Quinn," Jaxon said, looking uncomfortable.

"Good morning, Jax."

There was a long moment of awkward silence, then Holly cut in, "Catch ya later, Quinn."

"Sure," Quinn returned, softly. Jax just looked at her, but didn't say anything.

She watched them leave, feeling envious. Then with a sigh, she grabbed her can of warm cola and took a gulp just as the door opened again. Quickly wiping her mouth, she shoved the can out of sight.

A tall blond-haired man in a U.S. Mail uniform walked up to the desk and placed a bundle of letters in front of her.

"You're new here, aren't ya?" he asked politely.

Quinn smiled. "Just arrived yesterday from Los Angeles."

"Los Angeles?" The man snorted lightly. "They've had to resort to getting help from outside Hawaii now, huh?"

Quinn's smile faded. "Excuse me?"

"Didn't anyone tell you?"

She shook her head. "Tell me what?"

He looked at her curiously. "This place is haunted."

Seven

"Haunted?" Quinn exclaimed.

The mail carrier nodded. "Sure. None of the locals will work here. They don't even like coming here."

"Why?"

"Because of the ghost."

Quinn gave him a wry look. "A ghost?" She couldn't help it; she chuckled. "There's no such thing as ghosts."

Even as she said the words, she had doubts. How many times had she felt like she was being watched? And this morning, the guests were lighting up the switchboard with complaints of missing items and strange noises. One man even thought he saw someone in his room in the middle of the night, and he had found a torn piece of black cloth caught on the lock of his door.

"But you don't know the whole story," her visitor informed her, interrupting her thoughts.

"Which is?" Quinn prompted.

He leaned forward, resting his forearms on the counter above her. He appeared to be staying awhile.

"From what I've been told, Edward Barrington's granddaughter, Miranda Barrington, was killed in this place."

"Killed? How?" Quinn asked, intrigued.

"A fire." He shifted, and then went on. "She came to live with her grandfather about two years ago, after her parents died in a car crash. She'd only been at Barrington House for about three weeks when the fire broke out. She died in the blaze."

"How awful for the Barringtons," Quinn murmured. She looked around the foyer beyond the desk. "But this place looks great, like there was never a fire."

The man fiddled with a pen lying on the counter. "Only a small portion of the third floor was damaged, and Ed Barrington had it fixed up again real quick. He was open for business again a month after Miranda's death." He glanced at Quinn. "Rather quick, don't you think? No wonder the girl haunts this joint."

Quinn was thoughtful a moment. "Some people deal with the death of loved ones differently than others."

He pulled back abruptly. "You sound like a shrink."

Quinn smiled. "Thank you. I'm going to be a psychiatrist. I start university in the fall."

"Anyway," he continued slowly, "that's the story behind the ghost."

Quinn planted her elbows on the desk and rested her chin on her hands. "There's just one thing I don't understand. What about the guests? Why would there be any guests here if this place was haunted?"

"Do you think they advertise the fact?" he demanded. "You didn't know, so why should they? Then again," he mused aloud, "I think the word is getting around. This place hasn't exactly been bursting at the seams with people."

Quinn thought of the dusty unused rooms. "There's

no such thing as ghosts," she said again, but without much conviction.

The mailman ran a large hand through his blond hair. "Well, you just keep telling yourself that, little lady." He paused a second. "By the way, what's your name?"

Quinn sat up straight. "Quinn Hunter."

"The name's Jack Trainor." He stuck out his hand, and Quinn shook it lightly. "If you ever need anything, even if it's just a ride out of this place; give me a call." He grabbed a piece of paper from her desk and jotted down his phone number.

She frowned, thinking it odd that the mail carrier was giving her his number in the event she needed anything. Maybe he was just being nice. With a shrug, she took it, folded it, and stuck it in her pocket.

"See you around, Quinn."

Jack Trainor's story churned around in her brain after he'd gone, making it ache.

"There's no such thing as ghosts," she told herself, yet again.

"Talking to yourself, Hunter?"

Quinn jumped at Holly's voice. Jaxon was standing behind her, his dark hair wet and slicked back off his forehead. He looked great.

"You guys finished your swim?" Quinn asked, busying herself with something on the desk.

Holly smiled brilliantly. "It was fantastic," she exclaimed. "As soon as you're able, Quinn, check out the Barrington House private beach. It's excellent." Holly tossed her wet tresses over her shoulder.

Quinn glanced at her friend. "I think you got a little

burned." Holly had a pink glow to her skin.

"That's Jaxon's fault." Holly grinned at him. "He just had to throw me in the water before I could get any sunscreen on."

"You had it coming," Jaxon argued, finally speaking up. "You kicked sand all over me, and I *did* put on my sunscreen. The sand stuck everywhere!"

Holly giggled and slapped his arm. "Not *everywhere*."

Jealousy gnawed at Quinn's belly as she listened to them tease each other. Wasn't it just last night that Holly seemed so sorry about stealing the guys that Quinn liked? And what about Jax? What was that kiss all about? Both of them had short memories, Quinn mulled, peeved.

"See ya later, Quinn. Gotta get back to work," Holly called as she hurried toward the stairs with a wave.

Jaxon stayed behind, watching Quinn with his bright green eyes.

"What can I do for you, Jaxon?" Quinn inquired formally.

Jaxon sighed. "Are you mad?"

Quinn made a face. "What would I be mad about?"

"About Holly and me hitting the beach."

Quinn opened the register book and flipped through the pages, trying to appear busy. "Not at all, Jaxon. I didn't even think about it." At least that much was true. Jack Trainor had kept her occupied.

"When do you get off?" Jaxon asked quietly. He moved closer and looked down at her.

Quinn felt his presence, but didn't look up. Her heart pounded at his nearness. "Six o'clock."

He reached over and lifted her chin. She tensed. "It's you I like, you know."

Quinn's eyes widened. She didn't know what to say.

"Would you like to go out later?" he asked, his thumb gently caressing her cheek.

"Wh–where?" she stammered, her mind whirling. She swallowed hard.

He smiled. "To check out the sights. There's so much beauty on this island." The look in his eyes made her belly do a flip-flop.

She nodded, too afraid to speak, for fear he'd realize how much he was affecting her.

His hand fell away from her face and her chin dropped a notch, as if she'd been depending on him to hold up her head. "So, six-thirty then?"

Quinn nodded again. She watched him as he took the stairs two at a time, then disappeared around the corner at the top.

"He likes me," she muttered in wonder. "Me!" She laughed out loud.

Holly showed up at the desk just a few minutes before the end of Quinn's shift. "Hey, girl, how's it hanging?" she asked as she entered the reception area.

"All things are up and accounted for," Quinn returned, and then she looked at Holly suspiciously. "Why aren't you taking care of the dinner crowd?"

Holly snorted. "What dinner crowd?" When Quinn's expression didn't change, she explained, "I'm waiting for them to finish eating so I can clean up. Okay?"

Quinn looked at her friend wryly. "I seem to recall someone saying that *I* had the fun job."

Holly waved her words away. "So, doing anything special with your time off?" Holly waggled her eyebrows up and down at her friend.

Quinn was surprised. Did Holly know that Jaxon had asked her out?

"Oh, come on, Quinn." Holly hoisted herself up onto the desk. "Tell me where you and Jaxon are going?"

"You know about that?" Quinn asked slowly, warily.

Holly scoffed. "Of course I do. I couldn't shut that guy up. All he did is go on and on about you."

"He did?"

Holly nodded. "It was downright revolting."

They both laughed.

"What are you going to wear?" Holly asked excitedly.

Quinn shrugged. "I don't know."

Holly thought for a moment, and then suggested, "Wear the light blue skort and that cute white top you bought from Macy's."

"Okay, I'm easy."

"*Shh*," Holly hissed. "Do you want Jaxon to know that?"

Quinn slugged Holly on the arm lightly as she got up.

"*Owww*," Holly cried, rubbing her arm, her pretty face looking hurt. "I'm just trying to prevent rumors."

"Right," Quinn scoffed. "You'd better get to the dining room."

"Yeah, yeah," Holly muttered, hopping off the desk and heading toward the kitchen.

As soon as Edward relieved her, Quinn went up to her room to get changed. She was just putting the finishing touches on her makeup when she heard a knock. Giving her hair a final pat, she went to the door and swung it open.

No one was there. She made a face.

Odd, she thought as she shut the door. She could have sworn she'd heard something. She shrugged and went back to the bathroom.

She scooped up her clothes, and as she straightened, her gaze casually fell on the mirror.

Violet eyes widened and a moan caught in her throat.

Eight

Pretty...so pretty...

The badly scrawled words screamed out at her in her pink lipstick. A tremor tore through her body as the clothes she was holding slipped soundlessly from her fingers to the floor. She stared hard at the mirror until it began to blur and sway. Grabbing the edge of the counter, she tried to steady herself, but the room was spinning. Her knees buckled and she let herself slide down the wall until her bottom touched the floor. She blinked several times, hoping–praying–that the horrible words would be gone.

They glared back at her.

Terror gripped Quinn's belly. Someone had sneaked into the bathroom and written these words while she'd been checking the door. Was the person still here? Quinn's heart pounded painfully against the wall of her chest, making it difficult to breath.

With effort, she pushed herself to her feet and peeked out the bathroom door. "Is anybody there?" she called softly.

She held her breath as she inched out of the bathroom, into the bedroom. Her darting eyes scanned the room.

Nothing. No one.

Then something caught her eye. The curtains on the balcony doors moved softly. Quinn headed toward them slowly, her breathing erratic. Was someone out there? Just waiting for her? The white curtains fanned out gently as she reached the glass doors. She curled her fingers around a handful of material and began to pull.

Someone suddenly banged at the door. Quinn recoiled, crying out. She stumbled on a wicker chair, tumbling to the floor with a bang.

"*Quinn,*" a voice cried. It was Jaxon. The pounding on the door became insistent. "Quinn! Damn it, are you all right?"

The doorknob rattled as Jaxon tried the door. It swung open.

Quinn was struggling to her feet just as Jaxon reached her side. He grabbed her hands and pulled her up.

His eyes were wild as they bore into hers. "What happened? I heard a loud crash."

The curtains puffed out around them, drawing Quinn's attention. She shuddered.

"Someone was in my room," she muttered, her lips tight.

He looked startled. "What? Did you see him?"

Quinn shook her head. "I just heard–I mean–in the bathroom–he was there–and out here..." She pointed at the balcony.

Jaxon stared at her in confusion. "What are you talking about? Did he go out the balcony doors?"

Quinn nodded again. "I mean, I think so. I don't

know!" She tried to pull away from him, but stumbled, forcing him to steady her.

"Sit down," he ordered, leading her to her bed.

Just as her bottom connected with the mattress, she felt her legs give way completely. Her body began to shake; and shock tremors skittered down her spine.

Jaxon went to the balcony and whipped aside the curtains. Quinn jerked, expecting to see someone standing there, but, of course, no one was there.

Jaxon stepped out onto the wooden floor of the balcony, stooped, picked something up, and then returned to her side. "Does this belong to you or Holly?" He held out his hand, and in it was a small torn scrap of black cloth. The sudden fear in her violet eyes as she stared up at him brought him to a crouch at her knees. "We have to tell someone, Quinn."

"There's more," she whispered tremulously.

"More?"

She pointed toward the bathroom. "In the bathroom– on the mirror."

Puzzled, Jaxon rose to his feet and went to the bathroom. A few moments later he returned, his face grim. He took her by the hands and pulled her to her feet. "Come on, we're going to see Mr. Barrington."

She allowed him to pull her to the door, then she held back, stopping him.

"What's wrong?" he demanded.

"We can't."

A frown furrowed Jaxon's handsome brow. "Can't what? Tell the owner?"

Her head bobbed a *yes*.

"Quinn," Jaxon said softly, "someone was in your room. You have to report it."

She pulled away from him. "I can't, Jax. I'll lose my job."

"Lose your job!" He had to shake himself, his expression incredulous. "You obviously walked in on a burglar; you could have been hurt."

"I don't think I walked in on anyone." She hugged herself. "I think someone managed to get in here, though I can't imagine how."

"We *have* to tell someone, Quinn!"

She gave him a pleading look. "I can't tell Mr. Barrington, Jaxon. This is only my second day, I don't want to cause trouble." At his look, Quinn went on hurriedly. "I must have left the door open. Maybe the guy just came in here by accident, or maybe it was a joke."

"And wrote the words 'Pretty...so pretty' on your bathroom mirror? Some joke." He snorted derisively.

She touched Jaxon's arm gently. "Please, don't tell anyone about this."

His green eyes met her violet ones. "What about Holly?"

She shook her head. "Not even her."

"But she's your friend. She has the right to know some nut broke into her room."

Quinn shivered at his words. "She can't know."

For a moment, he just stared at her, and then said, "Quinn, I know this probably isn't the best time to say this, but..."

"But what?" she prompted, tucking a stray curl

shakily behind her ear.

"Holly and I heard something while we were at the beach."

"Yes?" she urged when he didn't continue.

He hesitated. Then, "Some guy told us that this place was haunted."

"Haunted?" Quinn tried to sound wry. "And you believed him?"

Jaxon shrugged. "I don't know. My mom did say that she was missing her silver hairbrush and mirror set this morning. And she swears she left them on the bathroom counter by the sink."

"She called me about that this morning," Quinn admitted distractedly. "But that doesn't mean that Barrington House is haunted."

He shrugged again. "The guy told me about Mr. Barrington's granddaughter Miranda." Jaxon related the same story that Quinn had heard earlier from the mail carrier, Jack Trainor.

She felt a shiver race up her spine. "What did this guy look like?" she asked.

Jaxon frowned. "I don't know; kind of blond, with blue eyes and rough features. And he wore a postal uniform."

Jack Trainor, Quinn thought wildly. What was he doing down at the Barrington House private beach? And why was he telling everyone that ghost story? Was he trying to scare people away from Barrington House?

"Quinn, are you all right?" Jaxon asked, concerned. "You look a little pale." He tossed the scrap of black cloth on Holly's bed and reached for Quinn, helping her to sit down.

She grabbed the piece of cloth as she sat down, gripping it tightly in her hand.

He expelled a harsh breath. "I knew I shouldn't have told you about this place being haunted."

"It's–it's not that," Quinn tried to assure him, her eyes looking like two huge bruises on her face.

"Then what?"

She shrugged. "I guess the break-in shook me up more than I thought."

His look was scolding. "I still think you should tell someone about this."

"No."

He sighed. "I'm going against my better judgment, but I'll do as you ask." He stuck out his hand to her. "Let's get out of here."

She discreetly stuffed the cloth deep into her pocket, then took his hand and got up. "I have to wash the mirror before we leave," she said, turning toward the bathroom. Jaxon stopped her with a hand on her arm.

"I'll take care of it," he insisted. "Just wait here."

What is going on in this place? Quinn wondered as soon as she was alone. Could Jack Trainor be right? Was Barrington House haunted? *No way, that would be crazy. That was no ghost who'd come in here; she had the proof.* She felt the small lump in her pocket.

"Well, that's done," Jaxon announced as he returned from the bathroom. "Let's blow this joint."

Quinn tried to smile. "I'm with you."

They didn't speak until they were outside in the garden. They sat down on one of the marble benches. It would be dark soon, but the moon was bright in the clear sky. The garden around them was artfully arranged and the smells were wondrous, teasing their senses. Tall lamps were flickering to life as night fell, illuminating the area softly, sweetly.

Quinn glanced up, seeing her balcony just overhead. Had it been only last night that she'd been dangling from the railing? She shivered.

"Quinn?"

Startled, she glanced at Jaxon. He was frowning.

"You know, since I met you, things have been...well, strange."

Quinn blushed. "I'm sorry, Jax. If you'd rather not see me, I'll understand."

"No! It's not that," he insisted. "It's just that I've never met anyone like you before."

She looked away, her gaze falling on a pink rose that was tickling her ankle. "I'm not sure if I should take that as a compliment or not."

He took her arm and got up. "Let's go for a walk."

He guided her down the lighted cobblestone path that widened at the end as it led toward the beach. It seemed strange that he knew where to go, but then he'd already been to the beach earlier, and this must have been the way he'd gone with Holly.

"Let's take off our shoes and walk the shoreline," Jaxon suggested, slipping off his shoes. Quinn followed suit, slipping off her sandals.

They walked slowly, wading through the water's edge. The moonlight danced playfully on the rippling ocean, as the waves lapped the shore, creating a feeling of peace.

"How long do you plan to stay in Hawaii?" Quinn asked, breaking the silence, wanting to talk about anything but what had happened in her room.

"For two weeks." He kicked at the water, splashing her.

She giggled, wiping the droplets from her face. "And you chose the illustrious Barrington House?"

He smiled at her. "It was my parents' choice. They're both business executives back home in New York City. They were looking for a nice small inn with little fanfare and even less people."

Quinn snorted wryly. "Well, they couldn't have chosen a better place."

Jaxon glanced at her. "Yeah, I noticed that. How many guests are in that place anyway?"

"Including you and your parents? About seven. Unless more arrived during Mr. Barrington's shift."

"Or left."

She gave him a wry look. They turned back as they reached the end of the Barrington property.

"What about you?" he asked.

Quinn smiled while she gazed out over the wide expanse of the ocean. "What about me?"

"How long are you here for?"

"Six weeks." She dug her toes into the sand with each step, enjoying the gritty feeling. "Then it's back home, and off to university. I'll be taking psychology."

His dark eyebrows raised a notch. "Psychology? I'm impressed."

They fell into a comfortable silence. For the first

time since she arrived at Barrington House, Quinn felt relaxed. Jaxon took her hand in his large one and held it lightly. She glanced up at him and smiled, tightening her fingers around his.

For some reason, as they drew nearer to Barrington House, her gaze was drawn to the balcony of her room. Suddenly, she stopped dead in her tracks, and gasped in shock and horror.

Nine

The light was on in her room and it silhouetted someone standing on her balcony, watching them. A cloak billowed softly around the person. A strangled cry caught in Quinn's throat and she couldn't breathe.

"Quinn! Are you okay?" Jaxon demanded.

He grabbed her shoulders and swung her toward him. His face, mere inches from hers, blotted out the horrible image on her balcony. She stared at him stupidly.

"Quinn!"

She yanked away from him, desperate to see the person again. She stared hard toward her room.

The light was off. He was *gone*.

Her eyes desperately searched each balcony, looking for the strange figure. He was nowhere to be found. Had she imagined him?

No. She couldn't have.

Quinn took off at a dead run, heading pell-mell toward Barrington House. She had to get to her room; maybe he was still there.

"Quinn, wait!"

She could hear Jaxon behind her, but she kept running. She tore through the garden, back into the building, and then up the marble staircase.

Holly was coming down the stairs, intending to go for a walk, when she saw Quinn and Jaxon speeding toward her.

"Hey, you guys–" Holly called, but Quinn rushed by her before she could finish.

Holly stopped Jaxon. "What the devil is going on?" Her hand gripped his T-shirt sleeve.

Jax shrugged. "I don't know. One minute we were talking and having fun, then the next–" He shrugged again, helplessly.

Holly bolted back up the stairs, with Jax on her heels. Their feet pounded on the hardwood floor as they raced down the hall. Holly's sneakers screeched a high-pitched wail as she and Jaxon stopped just outside the open door. She stepped cautiously inside.

"Quinn?" she called out. The closet door slammed shut, making Holly jump. She grabbed at her chest. "Damn you, Quinn! You're worse than that crazy cat for scaring the life out of me."

Ignoring her friend, Quinn went into the bathroom.

Holly tossed a worried glance at Jaxon, then followed Quinn into the bathroom.

Quinn was banging around in the cupboards. Holly frowned. "Are you looking for Buttons?"

Quinn straightened, her pretty face frantic. "No, no! A man!" Quinn opened a narrow cupboard, and then slammed it shut with an irritated cry.

Holly blinked with confusion. "A man? What the devil are you–" She broke off suddenly, then asked, "Quinn, I'm a little lost here. Do you honestly expect to find a full grown man in the cupboards of the bathroom?

Cupboards, I might add, that aren't even big enough to hold a bar of soap."

Quinn shot Holly a look that should have frozen her where she stood.

Holly shook her head as Quinn bolted from the bathroom. She tagged along and found Quinn stretched out on the floor, looking under the beds. For a moment, she watched Quinn, then strolled over to sit in the white wicker chair near the balcony doors. She waved Jaxon into the room, and he entered reluctantly.

Jaxon crouched down beside Quinn and put a hand on her arm, only to jerk it back when she jumped. He stood up again. "Quinn, there's no one here," he said softly.

Quinn pushed herself onto her knees, wiping a limp hand across her brow. "But I saw him, Jax," she whispered.

Jaxon tossed a glance at Holly, who threw up her hands in defeat. He put out his hand to Quinn. "Come on, Quinn. Let me help you up."

A strange, uncertain look filled her eyes as she stared at his outstretched hand. Then hesitantly, she took it. He pulled her up, and together they sat on Quinn's bed. For a long time no one said a word. Holly and Jaxon just watched Quinn, waiting.

Holly finally got tired of the waiting and spoke up. "What just happened here, Quinn?"

"Someone was in our room."

Holly's blonde brows raised a notch. "Excuse me?"

"Out there." Quinn tried to point, but her hand fell uselessly by her side. "On the balcony."

Holly jumped up and pulled the curtains aside. The glass doors were securely locked. She glanced back at Quinn. "The doors are locked."

Annoyance flitted across Quinn's face. "So? He could have locked them when he took off."

"Why bother?"

"I don't know, Hol! Why do we do anything we do?"

"I knew we should have told Mr. Barrington about the earlier break-in," Jaxon put in.

His words drew Holly's gaze like a magnet. "What break-in?" she demanded.

"Jaxon, you promised not to tell," Quinn snapped, glaring at him.

"Excuse me, but this is my room, too," Holly shouted back.

Ignoring Quinn's glare, Jaxon revealed all. "Someone broke in here earlier when Quinn was getting ready to go out with me. Somehow he slipped past her when she was checking out a noise at the door, and wrote a few words on the mirror."

"What words?" Holly asked as she headed for the bathroom.

"'Pretty...so pretty,'" Jaxon called after her. "But they're not there now. I washed them off."

Holly halted. "Why would you do that?" she demanded. "It was evidence."

"I told him to do it," Quinn put in.

Shock etched Holly's features. "Quinn, have you lost your mind?" She held up her hand. "No, don't answer that. You have. You've gone completely and utterly insane! Why didn't you tell someone?"

"I didn't want to cause any trouble. I was afraid we'd lose our jobs."

"Who cares," Holly yelled. "Some nut-bar was in our room, writing weird messages on our mirror, and you're worried about us losing our jobs!"

Silence filled the room as Holly angrily paced in front of Quinn and Jaxon, quietly mumbling to herself. Suddenly, she stopped.

"Maybe you're right, Quinn. Maybe we should keep the break-ins to ourselves," Holly said, thoughtfully.

"What?" Jaxon shouted. His gaze went back and forth between the two girls. "You just said you didn't care if you lost your job."

"I don't," Holly returned. "I have an idea."

Jaxon looked skeptical, and Quinn said nothing.

"Which is?" Jaxon prodded.

"We trap him."

Jaxon blinked, then blinked a few more times, stunned. "That's the craziest thing I've ever heard. It would be dangerous. Just tell Edward Barrington," Jaxon pleaded. "He can call the police. Let them take care of this."

Quinn finally spoke up. "I think Jaxon might be right, Hol. Maybe we should just take our chances and tell the Barringtons."

Holly looked disgusted. "Just five minutes ago you were adamant about not telling Eddie and Edith, and now you've miraculously changed your mind?"

"One could say the same about you," Quinn returned. "You wanted to tell someone, and now you don't. We're both on the same wave length, just not at the same time."

"Oh, man," Jaxon snapped, finally hearing enough. "*I* am going to tell Mr. Barrington." He got up and headed for the door. "Are you guys with me, or what?" he asked, stopping by the door.

Holly hurried after him, taking hold of his arm. "Come on, Jax. We can do this."

Jaxon wrenched his arm free. "Forget it. It's too dangerous." He opened the door and stepped into the hall.

"But what if I were to tell you that the guy who broke in here might actually *be* Mr. Barrington."

"What?" Quinn and Jaxon chorused.

Holly pulled Jaxon back into the room, closing the door. "You swear you saw Mr. Barrington at the Hard Rock Cafe, don't you, Quinn?"

Quinn frowned. "Yeah," she replied evenly.

Holly sat down on her bed. Jaxon and Quinn watched her carefully. "Well, I just realized something. I've been noticing that Eddie has been watching us a little too closely. He's always around when I'm working, whether I'm in the kitchen or the laundry room. I even saw him watching Jaxon and me from a window when we went to the beach earlier." She shivered. "It gave me the creeps. It's like he's everywhere."

"He might just be watching you guys to see how you're working out," Jaxon put in reasonably.

Holly shook her head. "No way. I've had other jobs, and the bosses don't watch you *that* closely."

"Maybe he's some kind of pervert," Quinn supplied.

"You know," Holly began, waving her finger for emphasis, "maybe the story Jack Trainor told us about a ghost haunting this place was greatly exaggerated. Maybe the only one haunting this place is Edward Barrington."

Things started to appear clearer to Quinn. "You could be right. On two occasions I've seen someone in a black hooded cloak. The last time, right on our balcony. It would be the perfect way to hide his identity."

"But knowing this just brings us back to square one," Jaxon pointed out.

"Which is?" Holly asked.

"This guy could be dangerous," Jaxon said. "You've got to go to the police."

"And tell them what?" Holly demanded. "That we think our boss is some kind of peeping Tom?"

"He's more than that and you know it," Jaxon insisted.

"We have no proof," Quinn put in quietly. "We erased the words from the mirror."

"But we have the piece of cloak. And the police could question the guests about their missing items and sightings. Surely, these things would be enough for the police to start some kind of investigation," Jax returned.

"Maybe," Holly said, "but I think Mr. Barrington is too smart to leave any evidence that would incriminate him, so..." Holly glanced at both Jaxon and Quinn, in turn. "We have to catch him in the act."

Jaxon expelled a deep breath as he looked at them. "Are you sure I can't talk you two out of this?"

Both Holly and Quinn shook their heads.

"Well," he began, hesitantly, "I still think it's a crazy idea, but I don't want you two to take on Mr. Barrington by yourselves. So, what's the plan?"

"Plan?" both girls echoed.

Jaxon frowned. "Yeah, the plan. The one we'll need to catch Mr. Barrington in the act."

"Hold your horses, Jax, I just got the idea; I haven't had time to come up with a plan," Holly returned.

He opened the door. "Well, I'm going to hit the hay. All this 007 stuff has worn me out."

Quinn followed him into the hall, closing the door behind her. "I'm sorry about ruining our date. I seem to have a knack for that."

Jaxon smiled. "Nah, you're the most exciting girl I've ever met. Every time I'm with you; it's an adventure." He cupped her face with his hands, pulled her to him, and kissed her forehead. "Goodnight, Quinn."

She watched him disappear into his room, then touched the place where his lips had been. She smiled softly. "Good night, Jax."

Something touched her hair.

She could feel the gentle strokes…could hear softly spoken words, but couldn't make out what they were. Groggily, Quinn opened her eyes. Standing over her was a black shape.

Mr. Barrington?

Startled, she bolted upright, her eyes wild. Frantically, she switched on the lamp by her bed.

"*Hey*," Holly complained, shielding her face from the glare.

Quinn hardly noticed the pain of the light stabbing at her eyes as she scanned the entire room.

No one.

Had she only been dreaming? It had seemed so real. She could still feel where someone had stroked her hair, hear the softly spoken, garbled words. She couldn't have dreamed it.

Quinn shoved her fingers roughly through her hair, trying to rid herself of the weird sensation on her scalp. She had to remember that she'd had quite a scare earlier. And that she had fallen asleep with the conversation about Mr. Barrington playing over and over in her mind. She could have been dreaming.

Quinn expelled a breath she hadn't realized she'd been holding then leaned over to shut off the lamp. *Yeah, I must have been dreaming*, she concluded as she settled under the covers on her bed. There couldn't have been anyone in the room. He couldn't have gotten away so quickly. She would have seen him.

Then why could she smell a faint musty scent in the air?

Ten

Quinn was working at the reception desk the following morning, when she noticed Mr. Barrington watching her from the top of the marble staircase. She frowned. He didn't even bother to hide the fact that he was staring.

She watched him as he came down the stairs, his blue eyes studying her intensely. She suppressed a shudder. Could he have been in their room? Was he some sort of sicko–dressing up in a black robe and sneaking around the place? No wonder people were suspicious of Barrington House. One *would* think it was haunted with some weirdo creeping around in a costume. He disappeared down the hall toward the kitchen, and Quinn let out a sigh of relief.

At least things were clearer now. If it was Mr. Barrington, he would definitely be able to get in and out of people's rooms easily. And what about the missing things the guests had complained about? Was he a thief, too? What had she and Holly gotten themselves into? Maybe they should consider looking for other jobs.

Mr. and Mrs. Caine walked up to the desk, breaking into Quinn's thoughts. She smiled at the couple. "Can I help you?"

Mr. Caine nodded. "Elaine and I have to catch a flight home, so we're checking out."

Quinn's heart missed a beat. Where was Jaxon? Was he at least going to say good-bye?

"I'm afraid there's a problem at work that needs my immediate attention," Mr. Caine informed her, "so we'll be cutting our trip short."

"Of course," Quinn returned woodenly, a tight feeling gripping her chest.

"Oh, I should tell you," Mrs. Caine cut in. "Our son, Jaxon, will be staying on." She chuckled as she looked at her husband. "No sense ruining his vacation."

Mr. Caine smiled at his wife. "I promise you, dear, I'll take you to the Bahamas at Christmas to make it up to you."

Mrs. Caine patted his cheek. "I'm sure you will." She winked at Quinn. "Are we all done here?"

Quinn was having a hard time containing her excitement. Jaxon was staying!

"*Umm*," she cleared her throat a couple of times. "Yes, all done."

After the couple left, Quinn flittered about, humming softly to herself. Jaxon was staying, she thought for the hundredth time. She couldn't restrain the smile that crept over her face. Quinn glanced at the clock and through the corner of her eye, saw Mr. Barrington. She gasped.

How many times had she seen that man today? She'd lost count. And it wasn't even lunch time yet. It was so creepy.

Holly came down the hall with freshly ironed linens, and stopped by the desk. "How you holding up?" she asked, glancing over her shoulder just in time to see Mr. Barrington disappear into his office.

"That has to be at least the fifteenth time Mr. B. has been around here," Quinn commented.

"You see? It has to be him," Holly said. "He's not even trying to hide it."

Quinn nodded. "Yeah. And, if you think about it, that's kind of scary. Could he be that sure he won't get caught?"

Holly sat down beside Quinn. "You know what else I was thinking? I bet Mr. Barrington *started* the ghost rumors himself. It would be the perfect cover to his whacked-out, perverted, kleptomaniac behavior."

Quinn picked up the papers she'd been working on and shuffled them. "Well, as stupid as this sounds, that puts my mind at ease, because I was beginning to think I was losing my mind with all the sightings and strange noises. At least now I can put a name and a face to my madness."

"You already lost your mind, Quinn, you just don't know it yet."

"Hardy har har," Quinn tossed back. "I think I hear dirty dishes calling you."

By the end of her shift, Quinn was feeling jumpy. When Mr. Barrington showed up at the desk to relieve her, she muttered a quick, "thanks," then all but ran up the stairs.

She was unlocking her door when Jaxon's door burst open, startling her. She jumped back with a yelp.

"Sorry," he muttered, his face turning red. "I need to

talk to you, Quinn."

Quinn moved toward him. "About what?"

He glanced up and down the hall, then motioned for her to come into his room.

She hesitated, then went inside, closing the door behind her. "Is this about your parents leaving?" she asked, peeking around his room. It was strange to be in Jaxon's suite. It was so personal, kind of intimate.

"No, but it is an added bonus." He looked at her eagerly, like a small boy with a new toy. "Actually, I've been thinking about what you said yesterday, and it makes sense."

Quinn nodded. "It does to me, too."

Jaxon motioned for Quinn to take the wicker chair with its plush gold and brown cushion. "I think Mr. Barrington was in my room last night."

"What makes you say that?" Quinn inquired, as Jaxon took a seat on the bed across from her.

He leaned forward, his arms resting on his legs. "I'd just gotten out of the shower, when I heard what sounded like a door closing. The noise seemed to be coming from inside the closet, so I checked it out."

He got up and went over to his closet. Quinn followed. He opened the door, and Quinn caught a whiff of a musty scent. She drew back, wrinkling her nose. Jaxon stepped aside, and her eyes widened.

Inside was a hidden doorway.

Did her room have one, too? It would explain how Mr. Barrington might have gotten in and out so quickly.

"Have you gone inside?" Quinn asked, moving closer, her eyes taking in everything.

Jaxon shook his head. "Not yet."

She glanced at him and smiled. He smiled back. Jaxon reached under his bed, pulled out his suitcase; then dug out a flashlight. He shrugged. "I like to read under the covers, makes me feel twelve again."

She chuckled.

"Let's get going, but let me go first," he insisted, slipping by Quinn. "It might be dangerous."

He flicked on his flashlight. The bright beam bounced off the lattice boards and cast eerie shadows. Quinn followed him closely, not wanting to fall too far behind. She glanced over her shoulder, everything behind them had fallen into darkness, it was almost stifling. The pitch dark...the mustiness...the tight confines... Quinn shivered.

"Are you all right?" Jaxon asked, his voice sounding loud and hollow.

She jumped. "Yeah, it's just a little spooky in here."

They moved on slowly, the light shining on another doorway.

"This would be your room, wouldn't it?" Jaxon asked, holding the light on the door.

She held her breath, and then nodded.

"Let's check it out."

They opened the door and found themselves in Holly and Quinn's closet.

"So, I wasn't dreaming last night," she murmured.

"What's that?" Jaxon asked from behind her.

"Nothing." She closed the door. "Let's keep going."

They continued down the corridor to a dead end. At least Quinn thought is was, until Jaxon's light touched it.

It was another door.

She pulled it open. "This is the way to the third floor," Quinn said quietly, placing her foot on the bottom step and peering up the dim stairwell.

Jaxon frowned. "What do you mean? Isn't there a main staircase somewhere visible on this floor?"

She looked up the stairs again. "Nope, this is it. I think this was the original location. I mean, the third floor was mainly used for the servants in the old days. Maybe it was always hidden, so none of the guests of the original owners would mistakenly go up and mingle with the maids. If you know what I mean." She raised her brows at him.

Jaxon chuckled. "I think I get it."

He cocked his head to the side in thought and stepped around her. "Look, there's another door." He opened it.

Quinn stepped up behind him. Why hadn't she noticed the doors before? Then again, she hadn't been looking, and they weren't exactly easy to detect.

"I bet this doorway will take you to the rooms facing the front of the house," Jaxon said, inclining his head toward the dark passage. He shut the door. "Let's check out the servants' quarters first, shall we?" He raised his eyebrows and gave her a quirky look. "You never know what we might find."

Quinn shook her head as she followed him, and then took over the lead when they reached the landing. She headed for the first door on her right and opened it. The room was empty and darkened by heavy curtains.

"Nothing here," Jaxon stated as he flashed the beam around the room.

He was just about to move on when his light fell on a small pile on a desk in the corner of the room. "What is that?" He walked over to the desk, with Quinn on his heels.

She looked at the contents.

"Some of these things were reported missing by guests," she informed him. "And isn't this your mom's silver hairbrush and mirror?"

Jaxon examined the two items and nodded.

So, Edward Barrington was a thief, Quinn concluded. *But why?* She picked up the silver brush and turned it over in her hand. A shaft of light from the flashlight glinted off the bright surface. None of the items were of any great value. What would he need with them?

"I think you've got some proof now," Jaxon said, his face grim.

Quinn nodded. "I guess we do."

She put the brush back, and her eyes fell on a tube of lipstick. *Her* lipstick. The one used to write on her mirror the other day. She picked it up with a trembling hand. She hadn't even noticed it missing.

Jaxon's hand closed over hers. "We have to leave everything as it was. And we shouldn't be touching anything."

Quinn glanced up at him and nodded as she let him take the tube and replace it on the desk.

"Let's get out of here," Jaxon said softly. "The police have to know about this."

Quinn let him pull her toward the door, but then suddenly dug her heels in to stop.

"Come on, Quinn," Jaxon urged, trying to tug her

forward, but she held fast.

He let her go. "What are you doing?"

But Quinn didn't answer; she just listened. Was that breathing? She yanked the flashlight from Jaxon's hand and scanned the room, the light slowly touching everything.

Nothing.

How can that be? She *had* heard something. She had!

"Can we go now?" Jaxon inquired as he took back his flashlight.

She grudgingly turned toward him. "Yeah, I guess. I thought I heard something."

Jaxon grinned at her. "It's this place. It's creepy."

She returned his smile with a half-hearted one of her own, and nodded.

As the door shut behind them, someone slipped out from behind the long, dark curtain and stood silently looking at the articles on the desk. With a slowness that seemed almost hesitant, the figure picked up each item, then headed for the door. For a moment, the figure waited, listening to the retreating steps of the girl and her companion. Then, opening the door, the figure glided out into the hall.

"Are you ready to head back yet?" Jaxon asked, swiping at some dust that had settled onto his head after he'd bumped into the wall of the old passageway. They were back in the hidden passages of the second floor.

Quinn helped free him of the dust. "There's just one

more place I'd like to check."

"And that is?"

She grabbed his hand and pulled him toward a junction in the corridor. "I want to see if any of the passages lead to the main floor and the reception area."

"I'll go first," Jaxon said, taking the lead.

They quickly found the passageway and stairs to the main floor. Just from the short time they'd been nosing around, they were beginning to understand the layout of the secret areas. Jaxon suddenly stopped, and Quinn nearly crashed into him.

"What is it?" she asked, her hand on his arm.

"*Shh*," he hissed. "Listen."

Quinn listened. She could hear Mr. Barrington. It sounded like he was talking to someone on the switchboard.

"I know that one of the locals told you otherwise, but I assure you that Barrington House is not haunted and is quite safe," an unseen Mr. Barrington said. "Well, if that's what you want then we will happily refund the cost of your room." He paused. Then, "I'm sorry you feel that way, madam. Goodbye."

Quinn could hear him setting down the headphones hard. "Damn," he muttered.

Jaxon suddenly leaned closer, and Quinn grabbed his arm. "What are you doing?" she whispered harshly.

Jaxon slid aside a small panel and two tiny beams of light pierced the darkness.

"What did you find?" Quinn demanded quietly, still tugging on his arm.

"I can see Mr. Barrington," he whispered back,

peeking through what appeared to be holes in the wall.

"What? How?" Quinn stood up on her tiptoes, trying to see what Jaxon was talking about.

"This is some sort of peephole," he said as he stepped aside to give her access.

Quinn peeked through the small holes. She could see everything: Edward Barrington; the reception area; even a little beyond. Suddenly, she knew from where she was looking.

From behind the picture!

Holly had been right, the eyes of the portrait had moved. Someone had been watching them that day. *Mr. Barrington* had been watching them. How many times had he been watching her work in the reception area?

She suddenly felt sick to her stomach. Settling down from her tiptoes, she glanced at Jaxon. "Can you close that again?"

He shrugged. "Sure." He quietly slid the little panel shut.

"Let's get out of here," she said, then headed down the passageway.

Jaxon kept pace, and it didn't take them long to find their way back to his room.

"You seem a little quiet. Is there something wrong?" Jaxon asked. He batted at his clothes, sending a puff of dust up around him. He looked bewildered, and Quinn had to laugh.

She shook her head. "Nah, nothing's wrong. I think this whole hidden-passageway/Barrington-skulking-around thing is just a little unnerving."

He nodded. "Let's have a shower then go to the

police. I'm sure they'd be very interested in learning about Edward Barrington's weird hobbies." He frowned as he realized Quinn was staring at him oddly. "What?" he demanded.

"*Let's* have a shower?" she repeated, jerking up a dark brow. Quinn suddenly giggled, as Jaxon turned red. It was so great to see someone else uncomfortable instead of her.

"I–I didn't mean it the way it sounded," he bumbled. "I just meant...you know...that we each...oh, never mind," he finished with exasperation, making Quinn grin again.

He looked at her and snorted. "Pretty cruel, Quinn," he scolded.

"I don't know, I kind of like this," she said with a chuckle.

"This?"

"Being bold. Being risqué. Saying what's on my mind."

He smiled. "I'm usually like that, but for some reason you knock me off kilter."

She chuckled again. "That's sweet," Quinn said, then headed for the door.

As soon as she was in her own room, she went straight into the bathroom. Her toe caught on a sandal carelessly left on the floor and she tripped, banging into the sink counter.

"Holly, can't you pick up your blasted shoes," she grumbled, and then something caught her eye.

She choked back a cry. "Dear God, no!"

Eleven

No touch! Pretty...pretty.

Quinn stared at the words until her eyes burned and the words blurred. *No, no, no!* her mind cried over and over.

With a shaking hand, she lightly touched the mirror. Lipstick...again.

Her pink lipstick.

"Why is he doing this?" Quinn asked softly. This time she was going to leave the message for the police.

She ran to the door, the message whirling over and over in her mind. What did it mean? She went out into the hall, and then it struck her.

"No," she whispered.

She headed for the closet, raced up the steps to the third floor, and hurried into the room they'd been in earlier. The room was dark. Quinn flicked the switch by the door, instantly bathing the room in a soft light. She looked around and her gaze came to rest on the desk.

"No," she cried, running toward it.

It was empty! Everything was gone.

"Damn! Damn!" She pounded her fists on the hard wood until her hands hurt. What were they going to do now?

With a sudden surge of anger, she raced into every room on the third floor; searching for the objects, and coming up empty handed. Still angry, she went downstairs and met Jaxon as he came out of his room. He was freshly showered and smelled great.

"Did you go back to the third floor?" he asked, puzzled.

She didn't say a word, just took him by the hand and led him into her room, straight to the bathroom. She shoved him toward the mirror, and he stared in disbelief at the pink lettering. He tossed a look at her over his shoulder, then spun around and grabbed her by the arm, pulling her out of the room.

"We're going to the police, right now."

Quinn yanked back, pulling herself free. "We can't," she said, no emotion in her voice.

He gave her a scolding look. "Oh, no, you don't. You have all the proof you need."

Quinn walked wearily over to her bed and dropped onto it. Flinging herself onto her back, she draped an arm over her eyes. "It's gone, Jax. All of it."

"Gone!" He advanced on her. "What's gone?"

"The stolen stuff," she informed him from beneath her arm.

"Are you sure? I mean..." His words trailed off as she slid her arm from her face and looked at him. "That's why you went back to the third floor," he finished for himself.

She nodded, pushing herself back into a sitting position.

"But what about the message on the mirror?" Jaxon

asked. "That's got to be worth something."

Quinn snorted. "Yeah, something."

Jaxon plopped down beside her with a sigh. "Now what?"

Quinn shrugged. "I don't know. We tell Holly what happened, then try to figure it out from there."

She scratched her head...then her arm...then a spot on her back. She made a face as yet another itch tickled her calf. She cast a look of longing toward the bathroom.

"So, why don't you go?" Jaxon said, as if he'd read her mind.

"I really want to take a shower, but..."

"You don't want to be alone?" He waggled his brows at her.

She cuffed him on the arm. "I just want you to wait in the room. Anyway, didn't you say you already had a shower?"

He gave her a devilish grin. "But I'm a very dirty boy."

She pushed at him as she got up, and he made a big performance of falling from the bed. "You have a very dirty mind!"

He laughed as he picked himself up from the floor. "Go take your shower. I'll make sure you're not disturbed. At least no more disturbed than you already are," he added, and was rewarded with a shampoo bottle torpedoed at his head.

"Hey! That could have hurt," he called after her. "Don't you need this?" He picked up the shampoo bottle and placed it in the hand that was poking out the bathroom door. He tried to peek inside, but Quinn closed the door too quickly.

Chuckling, he went over to Holly's bed and picked up a magazine with the glaring headline: "How to find Mr. Right and keep him!"

Flipping open the front page, he heard the shower turn on. He was finding it extremely hard to keep his mind on the pages and not on thoughts of Quinn in the shower. He didn't hear the silent feet that came up behind him, just a faint *swoosh*, followed by blinding pain, then darkness. He sank to the floor; the magazine fluttered down beside him.

A pair of hands tugged and pulled Jaxon toward the closet, stumbling beneath his heavy weight. There was the soft sound of one door closing, then another. Then the sounds were gone.

Quinn stepped out of the shower and toweled off. Quickly dressing, she opened the bathroom door.

"Hey, Jax, I hope I–" She stopped abruptly. She frowned. Where was Jaxon? He said he'd wait for her– watch out for her. She bit her lip. Maybe she'd overdone it a bit with her bluntness. Maybe he was mad at her.

She hurriedly dried her hair, careful not to look at the words scrawled on the mirror. She'd leave them for Holly to see. It's possible they might be enough evidence for the police, but she'd ask Holly first.

Quinn went next door to Jaxon's room and knocked. She waited, listening. Then knocked again. She frowned. He must *really* be mad at her. She'd have to apologize.

She made her way downstairs and found Holly with her head bent over a long white paper, writing something.

"Busy?" Quinn asked. She laughed when Holly

jumped and her pen skittered across the page, leaving a long mark.

"Thanks a lot," Holly snapped, pushing a blonde lock out of her eyes. "Now, I'll have to rewrite this." She gave Quinn a dirty look as she snagged a fresh sheet of paper and began to write again.

"Whatcha doing?" Quinn asked, leaning her elbows on the counter above the desk. "You don't work the reception desk until next week."

"Mr. Barrington asked me to fill out a complaint form from a guest before I call it a night," Holly said without lifting her head.

"Which guest made the complaint?" Quinn inquired.

"The older lady from Room 4 is adamant that the place is haunted; not to mention that the ghost is a thief. She's missing a pair of stockings." Holly finally glanced up, a wry look on her face. "Like who'd want some old lady's pantyhose."

Quinn laughed. "Mr. Barrington is getting kinky now."

Holly laughed, too. "Eddie in Mrs. O'Grady's pantyhose–" Holly shuddered. "Paints a pretty ugly picture."

"Have you seen Jaxon?" Quinn asked, hoping her question sounded casual.

"Nope. Thought he was with you."

Quinn didn't answer.

With the job done, Holly got up to put the form away. "Bored, are we?"

Quinn shook her head. "No, not really. I just have some disturbing news."

Holly cocked a brow. "More disturbing than Eddie Barrington–the human shadow?"

"Worse."

Holly sat down at the desk again. "So, what's up?"

Quinn glanced around, and then lowered her voice as she filled Holly in on Jaxon's discovery of the passageways; the stolen objects; the message on the mirror; and finally, the loss of the stolen items.

"Wow," Holly marveled. "You guys were busy." Leaning back in her chair, she sighed. "Well, we had everything, and now we have nothing."

Quinn frowned. "And the message?"

"It might help."

"Especially if Eddie left some fingerprints. Do you think we should try to go to the police with what we have?"

Holly's lips puckered as she thought. "Well, wouldn't his fingerprints be all over the hotel? He does own it."

Quinn sighed, deflated. "Yeah."

"And even if we managed to convince the police to come, Mr. Barrington might stop doing what he does so well."

"And this is a bad thing?" Quinn asked.

"Not really, but–"

"But what?" Quinn asked wryly.

"His stopping will only be temporary. He'll start up again. The man is sick, Quinn, he needs help before someone gets hurt. You of all people should be sympathetic to that."

"Yeah, yeah, I know." Quinn gave a heavy sigh as she rotated her shoulder, still a little stiff from her wild ride on the balcony. She tilted her head back and stared at the ceiling.

"All right then, we have to keep using ourselves as bait, and we need some kind of plan," Quinn mused out loud. "So, what shall we do, O Great One?"

Holly made a face. "Very funny." She reached across the desk, picked up a pen, and fiddled with it. She clicked it open, then shut, open, shut–

The clicking began to grate on Quinn's nerves. "Do you have to do that?"

"Do what?"

Quinn frowned. "Click that pen."

"Oh." Holly glanced at it. "It helps me think."

"You've got to be kidding." Quinn returned dryly. "So, tell me, have you come up with anything?"

Holly sighed. "No."

Quinn rolled her eyes. "It was probably all that clicking."

Holly made a face at her. "Oh, shut up."

"I'll catch you later, Hol, I'm going for a walk."

Just as Quinn turned to leave, she caught sight of Edward Barrington. She discreetly tried to get Holly's attention. When that failed, she tugged on a lock of her friend's hair.

"*Oww*," Holly yipped, rubbing her scalp. "Why'd you–" Her words broke off as she too saw Mr. Barrington. She gave Quinn a disgusted look. "He's coming *back* to the reception desk. You know; to work."

Quinn made an apologetic face. "Oh, right, sorry."

"Go for your walk, will you?" Holly scolded, massaging her head again.

Once she was outside, Quinn slowly walked around the garden. What were they going to do? How did you trap a man like Edward Barrington?

With a sigh she glanced at her watch. It was eight-thirty p.m. The kitchen would be closed, but maybe there was still something she could eat.

She headed into the house, making a beeline for the kitchen. It was empty, but the smell of food was still in the air, making Quinn's stomach rumble.

"Quiet, you beast," she scolded her flat belly as she patted it.

She went over to the fridge and looked into a plastic container: stew. Again? Discouraged, she looked into another container: boiled potatoes. Then, another: peas and carrots. Finally, she glanced over at the stove and noticed the big black pot still sitting on one of the elements. She went over to the stove and opened the lid to the pot. An odd smell assailed her nose. Picking up a large spoon that lay nearby, she stirred the weird, white liquid.

Suddenly, a face bobbed to the surface of the milky broth. A pair of wide green eyes stared accusingly at her.

Then...darkness.

Twelve

"Quinn? Can you hear me?" a voice called from the fog.

Quinn couldn't lift her head; she couldn't move. Something cool touched her face. It felt good, soothing.

The voice called her again. Quinn moaned.

"I think she's coming around," a feminine voice said.

"Don't crowd her," a man's voice ordered.

Quinn opened her eyes, finding three faces hovering over her. Her violet eyes sought out the most familiar–Holly's.

"Holly," Quinn croaked out.

Holly kneeled beside her friend. "What happened, Quinn? Mr. Barrington said he came into the kitchen and saw you faint."

Quinn didn't answer; instead, she struggled to get up. A cool, damp cloth fell from her brow. Edward Barrington grabbed her arm and helped her to her feet. She pulled her arm free the moment she was upright, then leaned on Holly as a wave of dizziness engulfed her.

"Maybe you should lie down," Holly suggested.

"I think that would be a good idea," Edith put in.

As Holly began to lead her away, Quinn glanced over at the big black pot. The lid was back on, and Edward

Barrington was watching her closely. She looked away.

In their room, Holly gently helped Quinn onto her bed, and then she sat down on the edge. "What the heck happened?" she demanded.

The bedding felt cool to Quinn's hot skin. She snuggled her head deeper into her pillow, closing her eyes.

"Oh, no, you don't," Holly scolded. "I want to know what happened."

Quinn laid her arm over her eyes. "I don't want to talk about it."

"Excuse me? Just who do you think you are talking to here? Eddie?"

Quinn lifted her arm above her head and rested it on the pillow. "It was just so..." She shivered, at a loss for words.

Holly tapped her foot on the floor. "Come on, Quinn, the clock is ticking," she said, each word in time with a tap.

"All right, all right," Quinn snapped. "I saw Buttons."

"So?"

Quinn swallowed the hot, acidic bile that crept up her throat. "He was dead, Hol! In that big black pot! Cat soup!"

Holly seemed to turn green. "Somebody cooked Buttons?"

Quinn pulled her arm down across her face again. "Yeah. And it wasn't a pretty sight."

When Holly didn't speak for a long time, Quinn peeked at her friend. Holly had tears in her eyes. Quinn suddenly felt terrible for the way she'd unloaded the news on her friend.

"Listen, Hol–"

"How could anyone do that?" Holly cut in, her voice wavering.

Quinn stared at the ceiling. "I've been trying to figure that out myself."

"It was Ed Barrington," Holly insisted. "He must have been watching you. He must have known that you were going to the kitchen, and that you would check the pot if there was no one around." She slammed her fist against her leg. "There's no way that it was a coincidence that old Eddie just happened to be there to see you take a nose dive. The whole damn thing was staged!"

"Keep your voice down," Quinn hissed. "He might be right outside the door."

"Good," Holly said even louder. "Then he'll know that we think he's a freaking psycho!"

Quinn sat up and took Holly's hands in her own. "Listen, Hol, take it easy. I was the one who saw poor Buttons."

Holly shook herself free. "Who cares! It takes a really sick mind to kill a defenseless animal just to make a point."

"A point?" Quinn repeated, frowning.

"Don't you get it?" Holly demanded. "It's a threat. Edward Barrington is trying to tell us that he'll kill us if we tell on him."

Quinn paled. "Do you think?"

Holly stood up. "What else then?"

Quinn's eyes darted back and forth as she thought. "I

don't know."

"And as for that message." Holly stalked over to the bathroom and glanced inside. "Leave it there." A determined look glowed in her eyes as she gazed at Quinn. "Tomorrow morning before my shift, I'm going to try and find those stolen items."

"I already looked, Hol."

"So?" she demanded. "It can't hurt for me to give it a try."

Quinn shrugged. "Okay, if you want."

Holly's face was grim. "I want."

Jaxon moved his head, wincing as a stab of pain shot through his skull. Who hit him? What hit him?

He cautiously opened his eyes. He was lying on his side, on the floor. He glanced at his feet; they were tied with pantyhose. His hands were tied, too, he realized. He was tied up so tight, his limbs were numb. He squirmed around, testing the nylons. There was no way he was going to loosen them.

He heard a noise. Someone was in the room.

Jaxon watched as a person got up from a chair in the far corner of the dimly lit room and walked over to him. The long, black cloak the individual was wearing brushed along the floor.

"Edward Barrington?" Jaxon demanded. "You'd better let me go if you know what's good for you."

The person in black said nothing, just cocked its head.

"Do you hear me, Mr. Barrington?"

A strange musty odor wafted over him as the figure

crouched down beside him; the hood still shielded the person's face from view.

"This isn't funny, Mr. Barrington. This is damn well serious!" Jaxon tried pulling at his bindings again, and at the same time, trying to get away from the sickening smell that was coming from the darkly clad individual.

The person remained silent. Then suddenly, the hood was pulled off, exposing a face. Jaxon sucked in a sharp breath. "Sweet Jesus," he whispered.

Early the following morning, Holly dressed and got ready for her little hunt. She was bound and determined to find those stolen items; even if it killed her.

She frowned suddenly. What an odd thought, she mused. *Even if it killed her.* She shrugged it off.

Careful not to wake Quinn, she slipped out into the hall and went straight for the closet that housed the stairway. Within moments, she was on the third floor. She looked around, frowning.

"Quinn was right," she mused aloud. "It is spotless up here." She moved slowly forward. "Probably just another twisted area of Edward Barrington's psyche; like hiding the third floor stairway."

Deciding to start at the farthest room and work her way forward, Holly opened the door to the room on her right and went inside.

By the time she'd searched four of the rooms thoroughly, she was beginning to doubt that she was going to find the objects.

Holly sighed. "Just two more rooms to go," she said to herself. She opened the door to the second last room,

and her eyes widened with shock.
"What the devil," she yelled.

Thirteen

"Jaxon!   What are you doing here?" Holly cried, hurrying to his side.

He'd been sleeping, but jolted awake at Holly's voice. He rolled over so he could look up at her, his neck, kinked and sore. He groaned out his pain.

"I'm doing my imitation of Harry Houdini," he said irritably. "How am I doing so far?"

"Very funny," she returned in a scolding tone, grabbing his ankles to untie him. With his feet released, she held up the bindings.

Pantyhose. Mrs. O'Grady's pantyhose?

She leaned over Jax to untie his hands when she felt him stiffen and cry out to her. She swung around just in time to see an object being brought down toward her head.

Pain exploded in her skull, and she slumped over Jaxon's body.

"Holly," Jaxon yelled, rolling his body back and forth in an effort to revive her. When that failed, he glared at the person in the black cloak. "Why are you doing this?" he demanded as his feet were tied again. "Damn you," he cursed helplessly.

The attacker stopped suddenly and stared down at

him. Jaxon tensed, waiting. The figure grabbed Holly, dragged her to the other side of the room, then stooped to tie her up.

The harsh rays of morning light peeked in through the slightly parted balcony curtains and touched Quinn's face with its warmth.

Quinn's nose twitched as she slowly awakened. Opening her eyes, she stretched, making a lot of noise in the process. Surprised that Holly hadn't given her *what-for*, due to all the racket, Quinn glanced at her friend's bed. It was empty. She frowned as she suddenly remembered what Holly had planned for today and desperately hoped that her friend didn't do anything stupid.

After a quick shower, Quinn let her hair dry naturally, not wanting to confront the message on the mirror. Grabbing a pair of white, hip-hugger shorts, she pulled them on. Then to complete the ensemble, she drew on a scoop-necked purple top and a pair of white leather sandals. She knew she looked presentable. The outfit was pretty.

In the kitchen, she ate her breakfast, and then went to her workstation with only an abrupt "Good morning" from Edith, who was doing her best to look too busy to talk.

A few hours ticked by, and Quinn was dusting the reception area when Jack Trainor arrived with the mail.

He set a large bundle on the counter. "Still here?" he asked.

Quinn smiled as she set aside the duster and collected

the bundle. "Where else would I be?"

"Didn't take me seriously, huh?"

She slipped off an elastic band holding the mail together. "About this place being haunted?" she asked, slowly sorting the envelopes. "Well, don't worry, it's not haunted. At least not the way you think."

When he didn't respond, Quinn glanced up just in time to see an odd expression cross the mail carrier's face.

She opened her mouth to ask him what was wrong when he said, "I've gotta run."

Quinn watched him go. Shrugging, she went back to her sorting. A few moments later, she saw Edith coming in her direction. She paused what she was doing and waited.

"Where is Holly, Quinn?" Edith asked when she reached the front desk.

Quinn blinked with confusion. "I really don't know, Miss Barrington. I assumed she was working."

"Well," Edith began, her face mirroring her disapproval. "If you see her, tell her to report to me immediately."

Quinn nodded, swallowing hard. Watching the older woman head toward Edward's office, Quinn bit her lip with worry. "Where are you, Hol?"

The rest of her shift slid by slowly, and with each hour that she didn't see Holly, her fears mounted. By six o'clock, Quinn was so anxious for Edward Barrington to relieve her that she was standing at the edge of the reception area, poised for flight. As she saw his office door open, she tensed, waiting.

"Miss Hunter," he said as he came up to the desk. "I

understand your friend never showed up for her shift today. Do you know what became of her?"

Quinn frowned, his words confirming her fears. "I'm afraid I don't."

He pinned her with his unwavering gaze. "I see," was all he said. Then, "I need to run an errand, Miss Hunter. Would you mind staying on a while longer?"

Quinn wanted to say no, but the look on his face spoke volumes. He was furious. She pasted on a false smile. "Of course, Mr. Barrington." She went back behind the desk.

The moment he was out of sight, she angrily swiped at a neat pile of folders lying on the desk, sending them spilling to the floor. She stood silently staring at the mess and then snorted. "Well, at least I'll have something to do now."

She'd just straightened the last folder when Mr. Barrington returned. Glancing at her watch, she noted that it was eight-thirty. It took the guy long enough, she huffed to herself.

He stepped behind the counter. "You may go now, Miss Hunter," he said curtly.

Dismissed, she headed for the stairs. "I'm overwhelmed by his gratitude," she muttered with disgust. Standing outside her room, she forgot about Edward Barrington's lack of manners and got back to the problem at hand.

Holly.

With a trembling hand, Quinn unlocked the door and stepped inside the room. It was dark and empty.

"Holly?" Quinn called out into the darkness. She

switched on the light. Holly wasn't there. And it looked as though she hadn't been in the room all day. Her bed was still unmade.

Mr. Barrington, Quinn thought suddenly, a sick feeling creeping into her belly. *I've got to get Jaxon's help.*

She took off like a shot out of her room and pounded on Jaxon's door.

No answer.

"Damn," she cursed, slapping her open palm against her leg. Could he still be mad at her? She pounded on the door again. "Jaxon? Are you in there?" She grimaced when she still received no answer. "I'm sorry about what happened yesterday, but this is really important." She waited. "Please, Jaxon, answer me."

Instinctively, she grabbed the doorknob, rattled it, and the door sprang open. She jerked back, surprised. Why was Jaxon's room unlocked? Swallowing hard, she looked up and down the hallway, and then took a hesitant step forward.

"Jax?" she called as she flicked on the light. The brightness bathed the room. Everything was neat and orderly.

She walked slowly around the room then glanced at the balcony. Maybe he was outside and couldn't hear her knocking. A sudden jolt of hope filled her heart.

"Just what the devil are you doing?" a male voice demanded sharply.

Quinn gasped as she spun around, her violet eyes wide. "Mr. Barrington!"

Fourteen

"I've been watching you."

Quinn's heart leaped into her throat. "What?" she asked with a croak.

Edward Barrington's face was red with anger. "I saw you break in here!"

"Break in here?" she parroted dumbly.

He bore down on her, and she stepped back, keeping the distance between them. "There have been complaints of things missing, but I never would have guessed...." He let his words trail off, his meaning clear.

Quinn gaped at him, appalled. "You think *I've* been stealing stuff?"

He crossed his arms over his chest. "The evidence speaks for itself."

"What evidence?" she demanded, anger burning in her belly. "I was trying to see if Jaxon Caine was okay when he didn't answer the door."

"Perhaps he just wasn't in," Edward boomed, making Quinn jump. "You have no right in the private rooms of the guests. Unless, of course, you're cleaning, and I don't see a cleaning cart." His tone was clearly mocking, and he made a point of looking toward the hallway.

Quinn looked, too, though she didn't know why.

Maybe she was hoping for salvation–in a cleaning cart.

She shook off the stupid notion and spat out, "How dare you suggest that I'm a thief, when it's really–" She cut off her words with a gasp, covering her mouth with her hands. She'd almost said it was *him*. If she'd blurted it out, she would have really been in trouble.

Where is Jax? her mind screamed as her eyes darted around desperately. She needed him. How could she do this all by herself?

No Jaxon. No Holly. No anybody.

"It's really who, Quinn?" Edward asked softly.

She gave a startled cry, his words close to her ear. When had he crept up on her? She danced away from him, putting the door at her back for an easy escape.

He pivoted on his heel, his eyes following her. "Why don't you enlighten me as to the name of the real thief?"

"I don't know," Quinn returned. Maybe too quickly, because the look on Edward Barrington's face clearly said he didn't believe her. "Maybe it's the other one. Holly. Is she the criminal, Quinn?"

"No," Quinn snapped. "You know damn well it's you!" She wasn't sure who was more surprised at her outburst, she or Edward Barrington.

"Me? You think that *I'd* steal from my own guests?"

Quinn edged toward the door, a little at a time. "Of course it's you," she went on, knowing it was too late to turn back. "Jaxon, Holly, and I know everything, Mr. Barrington. And the police do, too," she threw in for good measure. How would he know that they hadn't reported anything to the cops yet?

He blanched at her words. "What are you talking

about?"

She kept inching backwards. "We know you've been watching us, stalking us." Quinn swallowed hard at his angry expression, but went on anyway. "You've been sneaking into our room–writing sick messages on our mirror."

He jumped at her, taking Quinn by surprise. He moved fast for an old guy.

He grabbed her arms, shaking her. "What did the message say?" he yelled, shaking her again.

Quinn's head snapped back and forth, causing a shaft of pain to shoot up into her skull. Her breath caught in her throat.

He's going to kill me! The words reverberated over and over in her mind. She didn't want to die. Not like this. Not all alone.

"Tell me what the message said!"

His face was close to hers, and she could smell cigarettes and stale coffee on his breath. She tried to turn her face away, but he held her still.

"Tell me," he snarled.

"It said, 'Pretty...so pretty,'" she ground out between clenched teeth, then wrenched herself free when he suddenly relaxed his grip.

He walked away from her, his head in his hands. "No, no, no, not again. Damn. Damn!"

Quinn took the opportunity to bolt. She ran out of Jaxon's room and raced down the hall. Edward Barrington's voice followed her down the marble staircase, demanding that she stop.

Yeah, right!

Pretty, Pretty

She took off out the front entrance, slamming the door shut behind her as she fled. She was going to run all the way to Lahaina if she had to. She had to get to the police.

Her feet kicked up loose stones as she tore down the driveway, and her lungs burned. Something had happened to Holly, she decided frantically. And Jaxon, too. She just knew it. Were they dead? A sob ripped through her chest, and tears blurred her eyes. She could only pray that she wasn't already too late.

Someone stepped out in front of her, grabbing her by the waist and dragging her to the ground. An animal-like cry tore from her throat.

"*Nooo*," she screamed, thrashing violently. She had to get away! Holly's and Jaxon's life depended on it.

A hand clamped over her mouth to cease her screams, and a male voice hissed in her ear. "Shut up!"

It wasn't Mr. Barrington–it wasn't Mr. Barrington. The words went over and over in her mind with blinding relief. She went still in the man's arms. The man didn't loosen his grip, merely turned her over. A flashlight clicked on.

Jack Trainor!

"If you promise not to scream, I'll take my hand away from your mouth," he told her.

He seemed to be waiting for her to affirm his directions, so she nodded, and he took his hand away.

She sucked in a deep breath, and then demanded, "What are you doing here? Are you spying on this place?"

"Spying? No. Investigating? Yes."

Investigating? Her violet eyes grew wide. "You're not a mailman–you're some kind of cop."

He got to his feet and helped her up. "Yeah, something like that." Still hanging onto her arm, he started to lead her away. "Come on; let's go to my truck to talk."

His big 4x4 truck was hidden just off the driveway under the cover of the trees. They climbed inside and he turned on the interior light.

"Man, am I glad to see you," she gushed as she slammed her door. "I think Mr. Barrington has done something to my friends. He...he attacked me, then he was chasing me–"

"Whoa there," Jack ordered, his hands spread before him. "Slow down. Mr. Barrington attacked you?"

Quinn nodded. She went on to tell him everything, right from the beginning. Jack sat quietly, listening, only interrupting once in a while to ask a question here and there. "That's why I was running," she finished. "I was trying to get help."

"That makes three," he muttered. He seemed to be going over something in his head.

Quinn frowned. "Three?"

He was startled at her interruption. "Yeah, a local girl went missing about three months ago. I was assigned to find out what happened to her."

"Missing?" Quinn suddenly felt ill.

"Yeah," Jack replied, looking toward Barrington House. "Old man Barrington swears the girl never showed up for work, but it's beginning to look otherwise."

A look of fear crossed Quinn's pretty face. "Do you

think he killed her?" she asked, breathless.

He looked sympathetic. "I don't know, Quinn."

"Well, Holly and Jaxon are not dead," she declared hotly. "I'm going to find them." She fumbled frantically with the door, only to have Jack yank her away from it, closer to him.

"Don't be a fool, Quinn!"

She wrenched herself free. "They're not dead," she cried, feeling tears well up in her eyes. "They can't be dead."

Jack held Quinn as the dam burst, tears spilling down her cheeks. All the pent-up fear and anger within her, finding release.

When she'd finished, she pulled away, swiping at her eyes, embarrassed. "Sorry," she muttered, not looking at him.

Jack sighed. "Don't worry about it, kid. You've been through a lot."

"Yeah? Well, it's not over yet."

Jack eyed her, his face serious. "No, it's not."

Fifteen

Holly groaned, her head throbbing. She moved, wincing at the stabbing pain. Had she been in some kind of accident? She frowned, peeking through squinted eyelids. Then her eyes widened.

Where was she? Why was it so dark? And what was that *horrible* smell?

Then it all came rushing back. She'd been looking for the stolen items and had found Jaxon tied up on the floor in one of the rooms; then–someone had hit her!

When she awoke the first time, she had found herself tied up and alone in a room. How could she have been so stupid to let her guard down? She was in that room for a long time until she was cold-cocked again. Now she was here. But where was here?

She tried to move and found she was still tightly bound.

"Holly?" Jaxon's whisper drifted from out of the darkness. "Are you awake?"

Jaxon! He's all right!

Before she could voice her relief, a soft breeze moved through her hair, and sounds of the night filled her ears. They were outside. How? When?

"Yeah," she finally returned.

"Thank God," he said reverently. "You've been out for hours. I was really starting to get worried."

His words startled her. "Hours? Are you sure?" she demanded, trying to see him through the blackness.

"Well, no, not of the exact time span, I was knocked unconscious again," he replied, "but it was long enough."

Damn! Quinn! She must be frantic. Holly struggled against her ties, but only succeeded in hurting herself. Tears pooled in her eyes.

"Damn," she muttered angrily.

"Don't bother," came Jaxon's voice again, "they're too tight."

Holly dropped her head in defeat, letting the dirt from ground rasp roughly against her cheek. Taking a few deep breaths, she tried to calm herself, but only succeeded in inhaling the rank air that hovered around her like a blanket. She wrinkled her nose with distaste.

"What is that wretched smell?"

"There must be a dead animal nearby."

Holly shuddered with revulsion. "That's gross."

A mosquito buzzed annoyingly by her ear and she shook her head, hoping to shoo it away. It landed on her bare arm and dug in.

"*Owww,*" she yipped, rolling on her side to squash the insect.

"Are you all right?" Jax asked.

"As well as any entree could be, I guess," she muttered with annoyance. Up until this point she hadn't noticed a single mosquito since arriving on Maui; then she remembered reading something about the pesky insects being a nuisance for hikers. Just where the heck had Eddie taken them, she wondered as another mosquito bit her.

"Damn," she muttered under her breath.

Trying to focus on something else besides being eaten alive by little vampires, she tried to get a mental picture of her surroundings. Holly could hear leaves rustling in the wind all around her. The leaves were touching her, closing in on her. Heck, she couldn't even see the moon! It was almost like the foliage was swallowing them whole, hiding them, like a bad secret. A sick feeling settled in the pit of her stomach.

"Jeez," she yelped suddenly, rolling her body from side to side on the ground, crushing yet another bloodsucker. She rubbed her shoulder against the ground, trying to scratch the bite. "Jax?" she called into the darkness.

"Yeah," came his disembodied voice.

"Talk to me." She could hear him rubbing what she supposed was his own batch of insect bites.

"About what?" he returned.

"Anything." She bit her lip, trying to think of something, and then she asked, "Did Mr. Barrington take you from your room?"

"From yours, actually," he answered. "And I think you should know something, Holly."

"Yeah?"

Jaxon made some grunting noises. "Gad, these mosquitoes are killing me." He took a moment longer then, "It wasn't Edward Barrington who grabbed me," he told her, "or hit you."

She frowned. "It wasn't? Then who was it?" Silence

followed her question. "Jaxon? Who was it?"

"I'm really not sure."

Holly frowned, annoyed. "What do you mean you're not sure?"

He paused for what seemed like an eternity then said, "I've never seen anything like it."

"It?"

He groped for the right words. "I don't know how to explain it."

"Try."

"I think it's–" He broke off, still trying to find the right way to say what he had to say.

"Yes?"

He expelled a harsh breath. "I think it's some kind of monster."

Quinn and Jack sneaked back into Barrington House. They had to get to the third floor. If Holly and Jaxon were anywhere, it had to be there or maybe in the hidden passageways.

"Do you know where you're going?" Jack whispered, keeping close on Quinn's heels.

"Yeah."

She shivered, and Jack asked, "Are you all right?"

Quinn nodded. "The air conditioning is just a little too high."

He chuckled, but said nothing more.

She led the way to the hidden stairway. The closet was dark, except for the hallway light on the third floor that lit the top few steps. Then a flicker of light penetrated the darkness. She glanced behind, and Jack shrugged, the beam from his flashlight danced on the walls.

"Be prepared. It's the Cub Scout motto."

Quinn snorted, then led the way upstairs. They checked each room carefully, but there was no sign of Holly or Jaxon.

"Maybe he's hidden them in the passageways," Quinn mused out loud.

"Passageways? Oh, right, the secret passageways you mentioned earlier," Jack corrected himself. "Lead the way." He waved her on with the flashlight.

Quinn was glad to have Jack Trainor with her. Not knowing if Holly and Jaxon were alive or dead had her stomach in knots, but Jack was keeping her on an even keel.

She led the way down the stairs. "There are doorways into the passages right at the base of these stairs. They're real hard to find unless you're looking for them."

There was no response. Quinn paused, glancing behind.

Jack was *gone*.

Alarm ripped through her. "Jack?" she called lightly. She inched up the stairs, and then picked up the pace to a run, skidding to a stop at the top of the stairs. "Jack," she screamed.

It was then that she saw him. A figure in black stood over an unconscious Jack Trainor.

Quinn's whole body began to tremble. "Mr. Barrington?" she called out shakily. "Is that you?"

The figure didn't move, just seemed to be staring in

her direction.

"Please, Mr. Barrington, don't hurt him. Don't hurt any of my friends," Quinn pleaded, taking a tentative step closer.

A large hood shadowed the figure's face, and Quinn wished she could see Edward Barrington's expression. It would be easier to tell what he was thinking.

"You can't keep doing this," Quinn went on. "You can't kill all of us."

The figure cocked its head, then said, "Pretty...so pretty."

Quinn stopped dead in her tracks. Mr. Barrington sounded strange; *really* strange. Was he disguising his voice?

The figure stepped over Jack Trainor's body and moved closer to Quinn.

She held her ground. Maybe she could talk her way out of this. Maybe she could talk her friends free.

"Mr. Barrington, the police will be here any moment. They know everything."

"No," came a strangled cry from behind Quinn.

Quinn spun around and gasped.

It was *Edward Barrington*!

Sixteen

Quinn couldn't believe her eyes. "Then who—"

Her words were cut short as the cloaked figure stepped right in front of her and pulled back the hood. A pair of blue eyes, and then a face came into view.

A horrid face!

The face of a monster!

Quinn opened her mouth to scream, but nothing would come out.

The monster stared at Quinn. "Pretty...so pretty," it said, and then reached out a deformed hand to her.

"Miranda, no," Mr. Barrington yelled, leaping forward.

Quinn dropped to the floor and rolled out of the way as Edward Barrington collided with the monster and the two hit the floor with a crash.

Jumping to her feet, she bolted for the stairway; her breath coming in small gasps, her heart pounding furiously. The toe of her shoe caught on something and she pitched forward. She reached out into nothingness, her feet leaving the wooden steps. For a split second, she felt like everything had slowed to a crawl. Then she hit the stairs. She tumbled and rolled all the way to the bottom. She lay there stunned, and then she heard something.

Slowly, advancing down the stairs was the monster. It was coming for her!

Struggling to her feet, she gasped, her body one huge shaft of pain. She pushed the door open and fell out into the hallway. Dragging herself to her feet again, she tottered forward, her steps clumsy.

She had to get away. She had to get help.

Stumbling and lurching, she kept going, reaching the banister of the marble staircase.

"Pretty..." came a voice right behind her.

Quinn spun around, a scream caught in her throat. She felt herself begin to fall again, but she felt calm, accepting. Like she knew she was going to die, and that was just the way it was supposed to be. She felt weightless, and time no longer had any meaning.

It was time to die.

Then something vice-like clamped onto her wrist, halting her in mid-fall.

Quinn gasped hard, stunned at the sudden jolt that shook her very being. She looked at her wrist, then at the monster holding it.

"Miranda," a voice bellowed.

The monster turned its head toward the voice; Edward Barrington's voice.

Edward stopped just short of them, his head bleeding just over his right eye. "Miranda, darling," he crooned, "let the nice girl go."

The monster looked from Quinn to Edward, then back again. Blue eyes penetrated Quinn's.

Miranda? Why does he keep calling the monster

Miranda? Quinn stared harder.

A woman. Just a young woman!

"Give the girl to me, Miranda." He held out his hand to her. "Please."

Miranda didn't move, she just stared at Quinn. "Pretty," she said after a moment.

Edward nodded vigorously. "Yes, darling, very pretty. Pull her up and hand her over to me, Miranda."

The young woman hesitated, then pulled Quinn from her precarious position, and released her. Quinn dropped to her knees, shaking badly.

"Now, come here, darling," Edward soothed, motioning to Miranda with his hands. "Granddaddy will take care of everything, I promise."

Miranda was about to take a step toward Edward, when someone yelled, "Police! Hold it right there!"

Quinn's eyes moved from Miranda to Jack Trainor, who was standing with his gun trained on Miranda and her grandfather. He didn't seem too steady on his feet, but his gun never wavered.

Jack flashed his police badge, and then motioned to Quinn. "Get up and come over here to me, Quinn."

Quinn did as she was told, feeling so relieved she thought she would faint. "Are you okay?" she asked, when she was at his side.

"I'm fine." He glanced at Quinn. "Don't worry, kid, I've been hurt worse and still got the job done." He smiled at her, and then turned his attention back to the Barringtons. "Now, move over beside your granddaughter, Mr. Barrington," Jack commanded, using the barrel of his gun to motion the older man over.

"Please don't hurt her," Mr. Barrington pleaded. "She doesn't know what she's doing."

The remaining guests in Barrington House had begun to appear in the hall, all observing the scene before them with wide-eyed fascination.

Edward pulled Miranda closer to him, as if to protect her from prying eyes. "Just let me take her back to the third floor, and then we'll talk," Edward offered.

Jack shook his head. "Forget it, Barrington. She's a suspect, just like you."

"Suspect?" came a feminine voice from the stairway. All heads turned toward Edith Barrington. "Who's a susp–" Her words broke off in a startled gasp when she saw Miranda.

"Stay out of this, Edith," Edward warned. "She doesn't know anything either," he added for Jack's benefit.

Jack merely looked back and forth at the brother and sister, then said, "Get over there with your brother, Miss Barrington."

Her earlier shock forgotten, Edith got huffy. "Well, I never."

Jack made an irritated face. "And that's probably half your problem. Just get over beside your brother and his granddaughter."

Edith's face turned red, but she said nothing further, just did as she was told.

"Please," Edward appealed, "neither one of them have anything to do with the disappearance of the local girl."

A knowing look came over Jack's face. "So, there is more to the story than you originally told the police."

Edward nodded. "Yes, there is, and if you let my granddaughter and sister go, I'll tell you everything."

Jack seemed to ponder this, and then shook his head. "I think I'd like to talk to them as well–especially your granddaughter."

"*No*," Edward boomed. "I told you she doesn't know anything!"

Jack shrugged. "Well, I think she does. So, why don't we go downstairs, say, to your office, where it's more private, and have us a little talk."

Mr. Barrington mulled over Jack's words, then reluctantly, he nodded. "Okay." He took Miranda by the arm and began to lead her toward the staircase.

"*Nooo*," Miranda suddenly cried. "Pretty! Pretty! Pretty!" She shoved away from her grandfather, and he teetered over the edge of the stairs, and then disappeared.

Edith screamed.

Edward's cries echoed throughout the hall. His body thudded down the stairs, making grotesque snapping sounds that seemed to go on for an eternity.

Then all was silent.

Quinn, along with everyone else, hurried to the top landing and looked down. At the bottom lay Edward, his body twisted into odd angles.

Jack pushed past the group and rushed down the stairs. Leaning over the older man, he felt for a pulse, and then glanced up. "He's still alive! Call an ambulance!"

Edith ran to make the call, hurrying past her brother and Jack.

Quinn slowly made her way down as well. When she reached Jack's side, she said, "We still have to find Holly and Jaxon."

Jack rubbed the back of his head gingerly and winced. "I know, I know, but where the hell do we look?" He glanced around as if the answer might present itself. "Maybe Miranda–" he began, and then broke off as he glanced at the top of the staircase.

She was gone. Miranda was *gone*.

Jack sprinted up the stairs. "Where is she?" he demanded of the guests. "Where did the girl in the black cloak go?"

The guests shrugged and murmured their confusion.

"Damn," Jack shouted.

"Jack," Quinn suddenly cried. "Come quick! Mr. Barrington is saying something."

Jack returned to Quinn's side, just in time to hear Edward speak.

"Mir...an...da," the older man rasped out. Then his head lolled to the side.

Jack checked his pulse again and exhaled softly. "He just passed out."

"We've got to find Holly and Jaxon," Quinn insisted, pulling on his arm.

"I can't leave him, Quinn," Jack said, his face apologetic. "I have to wait until the ambulance gets here."

A desperate look came over Quinn's face. "Then I'll go alone."

"No, wait," Jack called, halting her. "We don't even know where to look, Quinn."

"I don't care," she yelled. "I'll find them, even if I have to search the entire island."

"I'll stay with Edward," Edith interrupted, drawing Quinn's and Jack's attention. "And I think it's possible that Miranda might have taken the two kids."

Quinn's eyes bore into Jack's. "Maybe that's what Mr. Barrington was trying to say before he fainted."

Jack's official persona suddenly slipped over him like a glove. "I thought Edward said you didn't know anything."

She sighed. "He was just trying to protect me, just like he was trying to protect Miranda."

"Where would Miranda take the kids?"

Edith shrugged helplessly. "I don't know."

Jack frowned, deep in thought. "What happened to Meilani?"

Edith paled. "It was an accident. Miranda never meant to hurt anyone–"

"What happened to the girl?" Jack interrupted, his face unyielding.

The older woman swallowed several times, and then said, "She fell down this very same staircase and died."

"Did she fall, or was she pushed?"

Edith shook her head and shrugged her shoulders in a jerky fashion.

"What did you do with the body, Miss Barrington?"

The woman's shoulders sagged, revealing she knew that the gig was up and there was nothing left to hide. "Edward buried the girl in the sugarcane fields off Highway 380."

"Can you be a little more specific with the location? That's just a wee bit of area to cover," Jack said wryly.

She hesitated a moment, and then she gave him the

directions.

Jack was still looking over his notes when he asked, "Do you think it's possible that Miranda might know where Meilani's body was buried?"

"I don't see how–"

"But is it possible?" Jack persisted, watching, as the older lady seemed to ponder his words.

"I suppose," she answered. "But it's not like the location is in the backyard. You would have to drive there."

Jack thought about this then asked, "How old is she?"

"Twenty-one, I think," Edith returned.

"So she had her license before the accident."

Edith's eyes widened with realization, but then she countered, "But Edward's car wouldn't be able to get through the cane plants, so she would have to drag the two kids through the fields, and Miranda's not that strong."

"The weakest person can attain great strength with the right motivation, Miss Barrington," Quinn cut in. "Especially if that motivation is fear, and Miranda's afraid. When the local girl died, she was frightened by the trouble that followed. But her grandfather took care of it; he made it go away by disposing of the body. If she thinks of Holly and Jax as trouble, maybe she feels she has to get rid of them, too."

Quinn suddenly blanched, the depth of her own words sinking in. "Dear God, Jack, we've got to find them now!"

Seventeen

"Did you hear that?" Holly asked as she heard an odd crumbling sound. The mosquitoes had been attacking her with a vengeance and she had been thrashing around like crazy, and whenever she moved she could hear the sound of earth breaking up. She was completely still now.

"Hear what?" Jaxon asked.

"And that smell." Holly wrinkled her nose. "It's revolting."

He was silent for a moment. "I know I said I thought it might be a dead animal earlier, but I was beginning to think, you know..."

"What?" Holly snapped.

"Never mind. It was a stupid thought."

Holly jerked sharply as another mosquito took a bite out of her, then she felt herself slipping.

"Oh, my God," she rasped tightly.

"What?"

"*Oh, my God*," she said louder.

"*What?*"

"I'm slipping," she said, her voice trembling. The ground seemed to be disappearing from beneath her.

"Damn," Jaxon swore. "Don't move."

"I'm trying," she cried. "Jaxon!"

"Don't move!"

Suddenly there was a loud scream as the ground gave way and Holly fell. She hit the bottom hard, face-first, knocking the breath out of her with a whoosh.

"*Holly,*" Jaxon yelled. "Holly, talk to me!"

She moaned. She'd fallen into some kind of hole. She tried to move, but couldn't, the area was so small her shoulders were touching the sides. And dear sweet Lord, what was that *awful* smell? It was nauseating.

Something touched her cheek. It smelled horrendous. She was sure she was going to throw up. She tried to move away from it, but she had nowhere to go. It felt like...like…

Holly opened her mouth to scream, but no sound came out. Then her eyes rolled back into her head and consciousness slipped away.

Quinn held on tightly as Jack expertly maneuvered his 4x4 off Highway 380 into the lush sugarcane fields. Plants bent and broke beneath the truck's wheels as they pushed through the foliage. Some poor farmer wasn't going to be impressed when he found a road ploughed through his fields.

Their headlights danced off the stalks ahead of them, and Quinn wondered how Jack knew where he was going, because they were completely enveloped by the vegetation. Jack suddenly hit a bump that slammed Quinn sideways, cracking her head against the side window.

"Jeez! Watch it!" She cast a glare in his direction as she rubbed her temple.

"Do you want to drive?" he replied harshly.

She blinked a few times, and then said, "Yes, I would." He only grunted in response.

They drove on, and after a few more minutes, he slowed the truck and rolled down his window, his body tense as he listened for any sounds.

"Did you hear that?" he demanded.

Quinn strained her ears, but heard nothing. "Hear what?"

Then she heard it...a male voice. It was a very faint, but familiar, male voice.

"Help us!"

"It's Jaxon," Quinn exclaimed excitedly.

Jack roared off toward the voice. As the sound got louder, Jack stopped the vehicle and jumped out, flashlight in hand.

"Please, help," Jaxon called again.

Following Jack closely through the sugarcane, Quinn nearly bumped into him when he suddenly halted.

"Quinn," Jaxon exclaimed. "Oh my God, am I glad to see you!"

Jaxon was lying on his side amid the plants, squinting his eyes against Jack's flashlight

Quinn ran to Jaxon and knelt beside him, touching his shoulder. "You and me both." She smiled hugely at him.

"I couldn't believe it when I heard a vehicle," Jaxon rushed out. "How did you find us?"

"There's a huge stone just to the right of you," Jack said, distractedly. "It was a landmark in the directions Miss Barrington gave me." Jack was frowning as he scanned the area. "Where's the girl?"

"Holly?" Jaxon asked. "I don't know, I couldn't see where she was. But, you have to find her quick, something's wrong. She cried out, then went silent just before you arrived."

Jack shone his light around, and something caught his eye. He moved toward it.

"Sweet Jesus," Jack murmured. He sprinted then dropped to his knees.

Quinn glanced at Jaxon, then hurried after Jack. She came up beside him and gasped at the sight that greeted her... and the smell!

From where she was standing, she could see Holly lying in a newly dug grave. Her hands were bound behind her back and she was lightly covered in loose mud, and just beneath her...

A *skeleton*!

Gripping his flashlight between his teeth, Jack grabbed Holly by the upper arms and pulled. He struggled with her a moment, then glanced at Quinn. "Can you give me a hand, Quinn?" he asked, the flashlight muffling his words.

Wrinkling her nose at the wretched smell, the two of them tugged on Holly and gently pulled her unconscious form out of the grave.

Quinn crouched down beside her friend, untying her hands, then her feet; while Jack returned to Jaxon's side to free him.

"Holly?" Quinn called softly. She patted her friend's cheek. "Can you hear me, Hol?"

Holly stirred and moaned. Jack came up behind

Quinn, followed by a slow-moving Jaxon.

"Damn," Jaxon muttered as he surveyed the scene beside Holly.

"You said it, kid," Jack put in.

Holly groaned again, and then her eyelids flickered opened. She brought up her hand to shield her face from the glare of the flashlight. "Quinn?"

"I'm here, Hol. Everything's okay."

Suddenly, Holly jerked into a sitting position, her blue eyes staring at the partially exposed skeleton lying in the grave. The beam of Jack's flashlight cast an eerie glow.

Holly swallowed hard as her body began to shake violently. She could smell the stench of decay on her clothes, her hair, and her skin. How was she ever going to get it off?

"Oh, my God," she said, her voice trembling. "I think I'm going to be sick."

Jack tugged her lightly to her feet. "C'mon, kid, let's get out of here," he said as he started to lead her away.

"I can walk by myself," Holly insisted, embarrassed by all the attention. She pulled away from Jack and the world began to spin. She stumbled and Jack reached out to steady her.

"This is no time for heroics," he scolded, holding her tightly against his side. "Let me help you."

She leaned heavily against him. "Okay."

Jack guided Holly to the truck, with Quinn and Jaxon only a few steps behind. As Holly was seated inside the 4x4, her gaze locked with Quinn's. Quinn squeezed in close to her friend, allowing Jaxon to get into the cab, too.

She grabbed Holly's hand and held tight. She smiled a small, reassuring smile.

"It's over now, Hol."

Holly nodded, "We did it, didn't we?"

Jaxon placed his dirty hand over both friends' hands, and he smiled. "We sure did."

Miranda covered her ears against the high-pitched whining of a siren. She hated that sound.

She moved silently though the garden, hidden in the darkness. The area smelled earthy; the flowers, lush. The wailing stopped, and she made her way around to the front of the house and hid in a set of bushes, watching.

Her blue eyes scanned the front yard, until they came to rest on four people as they got out of a big truck and headed toward the flashing lights of an ambulance that was surrounded by four police cars.

There were so many people, but she zoomed in on Quinn.

"Pretty...so pretty," she whispered.

Eighteen

"I wish I could get out of here," Holly complained, shifting uncomfortably on the hospital bed.

Quinn chuckled. "Just one more night, Hol, and then freedom."

"Anyway," Jaxon put in, from a chair nearby, "you haven't missed much, except maybe the high-class hotel the cops put us in while they tore apart Barrington House."

Holly's face suddenly clouded over. "That...ah...dead girl," she began slowly, faltering. "Was she the one your friend, Jack Trainor–I mean, Detective Paul Grant–was looking for?" she asked.

With the case blown wide open, it was common knowledge that the name, Jack Trainor, had been Paul Grant's cover while he'd been investigating the Barringtons.

Quinn nodded. "Yeah, modern science is an amazing thing; DNA testing, dental records. It wasn't too hard to make the identification. Also, Edward Barrington is singing like a bird, though he's the first to admit that he doesn't really know what transpired between the dead girl and his granddaughter, Miranda. Fearing the worst, he felt that he had to protect Miranda from the world, and from herself."

"I can't believe that girl was the monster," Holly said sadly.

Quinn's mouth twisted ruefully. "Actually, Paul said that Miranda used to be a beautiful girl. She was horribly disfigured in a fiery car crash that killed both her parents. No one could believe she'd survived the accident. She was, by far, a miracle. She remained in a coma for months. Then suddenly just woke up. But after one look at herself, she went completely insane. They say they couldn't stop her screaming for three days. They couldn't calm her, and nothing could sedate her. They ended up just having to wait until she lost her voice. After that, it was said she never spoke again."

"But she did speak again," Holly said quietly.

Quinn gazed at her best friend. "Yeah, she did." Though it was more of a rasp, and all Miranda ever said was "*Pretty...pretty.*"

"Paul said that after Edward Barrington's granddaughter recovered, he just couldn't bring himself to put her in an institution, and instead, took her home to Barrington House," Quinn continued. "Not even after she tried to burn down Barrington House would he send her away. He just quickly fixed the place, and it was business as usual. But no one saw Miranda again after the fire, and it was rumored that she died in the blaze, and the Barringtons never corrected anyone."

"But she was alive, and he kept her locked up on the third floor," Holly said, sickened.

Quinn nodded. "He obviously didn't expect her to get out."

Jaxon snorted. "I don't know why. All she had to do was open the door and *voila*. Freedom."

"I don't think Mr. Barrington thought that Miranda had the mental capacity to get out. He must have thought it was a fluke that Miranda got out the first time when Meilani was killed," Quinn put forth, "and that it wouldn't happen again."

"Yeah, right," Holly remarked snidely. "Only it did, and we almost paid with our lives for that little notion."

Quinn drew her knees up and rested her chin against them. "I guess Mr. Barrington didn't understand what was really going on inside his granddaughter's head."

"Who would?" Jaxon commented, shaking his head.

"Well," Quinn began, "according to the psychiatrist who did a preliminary profile on Miranda for the police, he thinks that because Miranda's own beauty is gone, that she's looking for it in others. That she's drawn to pretty girls. That they are the epitome of what she once was. He also believes she's clinically insane and should be hospitalized."

Holly looked at Quinn. "What do you think?"

Quinn frowned thoughtfully. "I suppose that could be the case. I mean, all of the signs point in that direction." She shrugged again. "But I think the extent of Miranda's insanity could be questioned."

Holly frowned. "Why would you say that?"

"Because they never found her," Quinn returned simply.

"Are you serious?" Holly demanded, her pretty face shocked.

Jaxon's face mirrored Holly's.

Pretty, Pretty

Quinn looked at each friend in turn, before glancing out the hospital window. "She's still out there. And she doesn't want to be found. That takes some kind of self-awareness."

"That doesn't mean that she won't be found," Jaxon reminded her.

"And she should be found," Holly put in. "I feel real bad for Miranda, but she is dangerous. She may have killed Meilani, and poor Buttons too."

"Buttons?" Jaxon asked, confused.

"Buttons was the Barringtons' cat," Quinn supplied. "Somone turned him into cat soup."

"Cat?"

Holly shot him a strange look. "Yeah, a furry four-legged creature that purrs? I'm hoping you've seen one before." She chuckled in spite of herself.

Jaxon had a pained expression on his face. "Wait a minute. You're saying the Barringtons' cat is dead?"

Quinn frowned and nodded.

"Well then they must have two cats, because some crazy feline was hiding in my suitcase, and scared me half to death when I opened it to pack the other day."

Stunned, Quinn and Holly stared at each other. Then, "*Buttons,*" they shouted in unison.

"That's such a relief," Holly burst out. "I'm so glad to hear that the animal is all right."

"Says you," Jaxon returned dryly. "I have gray hairs now. And if that cat knows what's good for him, he'll stay out of my way."

Holly laughed. "Oh yeah? Do you want to know what that wingnut cat did to me?"

Holly and Jaxon went on to compare numerous Buttons stories, while Quinn just smiled and nodded. She tuned them out, having her own thoughts.

Buttons was alive and screechin', Quinn mused. She was just as relieved as Holly to discover this piece of news. The cat might be a royal pain in the butt, but it was a living thing and certainly didn't deserve to be harmed. So then what had Quinn seen in that big pot that day? Perhaps it was her mind playing tricks on her, but, she surmised, she would never truly know.

More so, since Miranda obviously hadn't hurt Buttons, then maybe, just maybe, she hadn't hurt Meilani either. A rush of sympathy coursed through Quinn. Miranda didn't deserve all that had happened to her, and still was happening to her.

Quinn sighed, playing with a silver bracelet she was wearing on her wrist. A beautiful gift from Paul for her acts of bravery. She'd actually thought the concept of the gift was a little silly, for she'd been anything but brave. She'd been terrified.

Maybe that was how Miranda had felt with all those people staring at her. Terrified. Their eyes seeing a monster instead of a young woman; not caring or understanding how she came to be that way. Maybe she didn't mean to hurt anyone. Maybe she was just reaching out for an ounce of human kindness in a world where outer beauty was everything, and inner beauty was overlooked.

"Maybe..." Quinn murmured to herself.

"What was that, Quinn?" Jaxon asked, leaning forward, his handsome face frowning.

Pretty, Pretty

Quinn glanced at him, and then shook her head. "Nothing. It was nothing." She let her gaze wander to the view beyond the window, and sighed again.

Epilogue

The beach was deserted, except for a single sunbather languishing on her stomach, soaking up the rays. Her skin glistened in the sunlight with suntan oil. Her dark curly hair was tucked neatly behind her ears. Her pretty face was resting on the curve of her arm, and her head bobbed lightly to music playing on the headphones of her MP3 player.

A shadow fell across her and she blinked her eyes open, her gaze coming to rest on the bottom of a black skirt. Her gaze slowly traveled up the intruder's darkly cloaked form and she couldn't help but wonder how the person could stand the heat in that get-up.

She pushed herself up onto her elbows, and slid the headphones back until they rested on her neck. Music could still be heard buzzing from the foam buds. The girl craned her neck, looking up. The sun, directly behind the individual, almost seemed like a halo surrounding the hood that hid the person's face.

"Can I help you?" she asked politely, shading her eyes.

"Pretty...so pretty..." the person rasped, repeating the words over and over.

The darkly clothed person leaned forward, extending

a hand towards the sunbather.

The girl jerked back. "Hey," she snapped. "What do you think you're doing?"

The hood suddenly slipped back, exposing a face.

A terrifying face.

The girl's blue eyes bulged to extremes, and then she began to scream.

Meet the author:

I was born and raised in Manitoba, Canada, where summers are hot and winters make you wish for the summer again. I have always loved to read and write. The first books that caught my imagination were the Nancy Drew Mysteries. I loved the way Nancy would always find herself in the middle of a mystery and of course bring her friends along for the ride.

I have to admit, writing about things that go bump in the night is always fun. Add teenagers, their sense of humor, and their sense of adventure and you have *great* fun! I had a great time writing **Pretty Pretty**, and I have a lot more creepy tales hidden in the dark recesses of my mind, just waiting to break free onto the pages of a manuscript. Ideas can be a funny thing, coming from the strangest places. One of the most common questions people ask a writer is: "Where do you get your ideas?" I don't know about anyone else, but my ideas come from a squat, gargoyle-like muse that sits beside me when I work and drools green slime on my keyboard.

Happy reading!

Also available from Echelon Press Publishing

True Friends (*Historical for Young Readers*) K.C. Oliver

The Great War rages across Europe, and in Memphis, tomboy Annie rages at the thought of becoming a proper girl. When devious Iris Elizabeth offers escape from household drudgery, Annie is tempted to forget her old friends who have become known as Huns. A deadly flu epidemic brings new challenges, and Annie must make a decision that will determine her future.

$9.99   ISBN 1-59080-420-1

Trails of the Dime Novel (*Western Adventure*) Terry Burns

Danger and excitement…In the late 1800's the imagination of a nation was fueled by the wonder of Dime Novels. Gunfights and showdowns…Rick Dayton is headed west to write the beloved stories only to find himself living them instead. The making of legends…Travel across the west with him as every new adventure offers another novel in the journey of a lifetime.

$13.99   ISBN 1-59080-386-8

Anna Chase and the Butterfly Girls (*Fantasy for Young Readers*) Jadan B. Grace

Anna Chase is thrilled to share the tales of the Butterfly Girls with her young daughter, Brandy. Stories of another time and place offer solace to the lonely heart of the young widow as she relives the triumphs and tragedies of the beautiful winged creatures. Day by day, Anna tells the story of the exquisite Lady Willow and handsome Baron of Butterfly Haven who triumph over drought and devastation.

$10.99   ISBN 1-59080-083-4

The Dreamer (*Fantasy for Young Readers*) Scott Matheson

It's bad enough being twelve years old, but when you're scrawny, and painfully shy, life is torture. To escape, William spends hours each day daydreaming, lost in the safe world of his imagination. Enter the Guardian of the Great Wall.

While on this magical adventure, William will fight incredible evil while discovering incredible truths about himself.

$14.99   ISBN 1-59080-235-7